REPUTATIONS

REPUTATIONS

JUAN GABRIEL VÁSQUEZ

Translated from the Spanish
by Anne McLean

RIVERHEAD BOOKS | *New York* | 2016

RIVERHEAD BOOKS
An imprint of Penguin Random House LLC
375 Hudson Street
New York, New York 10014

First published in Great Britain in 2016 by Bloomsbury Publishing
Originally published in Spain in 2013 by Alfaguara as *Las reputaciones*

Library of Congress Cataloging-in-Publication Data

Names: Vásquez, Juan Gabriel, author. | McLean, Anne, translator.
Title: Reputations / Juan Gabriel Vásquez; translated from the Spanish by Anne McLean.
Other titles: Reputaciones. English.
Description: New York: Riverhead Books, 2016.
Identifiers: LCCN 2016003535 | ISBN 9781594633478
Subjects: LCSH: Cartoonists—Colombia—Fiction. | Political fiction.
Classification: LCC PQ8180.32.A797 R4713 2016 | DDC 863/.64—dc23
LC record available at http://lccn.loc.gov/2016003535
p.   cm.

Printed in the United States of America
1   3   5   7   9   10   8   6   4   2

Book design by Gretchen Achilles

For Justin Webster and Assumpta Ayuso

Identical noses do not make identical men.

—RODOLPHE TÖPFFER, *Essai de physiognomonie*

ONE

Sitting on a bench in the Parque Santander, having his shoes shined before it was time for the tribute to begin, Mallarino was suddenly sure he'd just seen a long-dead political cartoonist. He had his left foot on the wooden crate and his back pressed against the cushion of the chair so his old hernia wouldn't start acting up, and he'd been letting the time slip past by reading the local tabloids, the cheap newsprint blackening his fingers and the huge red headlines telling him of bloody crimes, sexual secrets, aliens abducting children from barrios on the south side. Reading the tabloids was a sort of guilty pleasure: something he allowed himself only when nobody was looking. That's what Mallarino was thinking about—the hours he'd lost here, given over to this perversion beneath the pale sunshades—when he looked up, away from the words, as one does to remember better, and, finding his gaze met by the tall buildings, the ever gray sky, the trees that had been cracking the asphalt since the beginning of time, felt as though he were seeing it all for the first time. And then it happened.

It was just a fraction of a second: the figure crossed Seventh Avenue in his dark suit, untidy bow tie, and broad-brimmed hat, then turned the corner beside the Church of San Francisco and disappeared forever. In an effort not to lose sight of him, Mallarino leaned forward and stepped off the crate just as the bootblack was about to apply the shoe polish to the leather, leaving an oblong mark on Mallarino's pale gray sock—a black eye looking up at him accusingly from below, just like the man's half-closed eyes. Mallarino, who until now had seen the bootblack only from above—the shoulders of his blue coveralls speckled with fresh dandruff, the crown cleared by an encroaching baldness—found himself facing a veiny nose, small protruding ears, and a white-and-gray moustache, like pigeon shit. "Sorry," said Mallarino, "I thought I'd seen someone." The man went back to his work, the well-aimed strokes of his hand applying shoe polish to the instep. "Hey," Mallarino added, "could I ask you a question?"

"Go ahead, chief."

"Did you ever hear of Ricardo Rendón?"

Silence reached him from below: one beat, then a second.

"Doesn't ring a bell, sorry," said the man. "If you want we can ask my colleagues after."

His colleagues. Two or three of them were already starting to pack up their things. They were closing up chairs, folding cloths, putting brushes with scuffed-up bristles and dented tins of shoe polish away in their wooden crates, and the air, beneath the commotion of the evening traffic, filled with the sound of metal banging together and lids being screwed on tightly. It was ten to five in the afternoon: since when had Bogotá's bootblacks worked fixed hours? Mallarino had drawn them on a few occasions, especially in the early days, when coming downtown and going for a stroll and having his shoes shined was a way of taking the city's pulse, of feeling that he was a direct witness to his own material. All that had changed: Mallarino had changed; the bootblacks had changed too. He almost never came into the city anymore and had grown used to seeing the world on screens or pages, to letting life come to him instead of hunting it down in its hiding places, as if he'd realized that he'd earned it, that now, after so many years, it was life that should come looking for him. The bootblacks, for their part, ruled their workplaces—those two square meters of public space—no longer by virtue of a pact of honor, but rather by belonging to a union: the payment of monthly dues, the possession of a laminated membership card that they showed at the slightest provocation. Yes, the city was different now. But it wasn't nostalgia that overwhelmed Mallarino as he noted the changes; it was a strange desire to hold back the march of chaos, as if doing so would also hold back his own interior entropy, the slow oxidation of his organs, the erosion of his memory that was reflected in the city's stubborn forgetfulness—as exemplified by the fact that nobody knew who Ricardo Rendón was anymore. Ricardo Rendón, the greatest political cartoonist in Colombian history, who had just walked by despite having been dead for seventy-nine years, had been devoured, like so many other figures, by the insatiable hunger of oblivion. *They'll forget me too one day,* thought Mallarino. As he lowered his foot off the crate and raised the other one in its place, and as he shook the paper so that a wrinkled page would return to its proper place (a dexterous flick of the wrists), Mallarino thought: *Yes, they'll forget me too.* Then he thought: *But not for quite a while yet.* And in that moment he heard himself say:

"What about Javier Mallarino?"

The bootblack took a second to realize the question was directed at him. "Sir?"

"Javier Mallarino. Do you know who he is?"

"The guy who does the cartoons for the newspaper," the man said. "But he doesn't come around here anymore.

He got tired of Bogotá, that's what I was told. He's been living out of town for ages now, up in the mountains."

So there's something that was still remembered. It shouldn't have surprised him: his move at the beginning of the eighties, before the years of terrorism had even begun and people had fewer reasons for leaving, had been national news. Waiting for him to say something else, a question or some exclamation, Mallarino stared at the bald spot on the top of the bootblack's head, that devastated territory with the odd strand of hair popping up here and there, with marks revealing the hours spent out in the sun: potentially cancerous spots, the places where a life might begin to be extinguished. But the man didn't say anything more. He hadn't recognized him. In a few minutes Mallarino would receive the definitive consecration, the orgasm corresponding to a forty-year-long intercourse with his trade, and this had not ceased to surprise him: people didn't recognize him. His political cartoons had turned him into what Rendón had been in the 1930s: a moral authority for half the country, public enemy number one for the other half, and for all of them a man able to cause the repeal of a law, overturn a judge's decision, bring down a mayor, or seriously threaten the stability of a ministry, and all this with no other weapons than paper and India ink. And nevertheless on the street he was nobody, *he could go on being nobody*, since the caricatures, as opposed to columns these days, were never accompanied by a photo of their perpetrator: for the average reader out on the street it was as if they drew themselves, free of any authorship, like a downpour, or an accident.

The guy who does the cartoons. Yes, that was Mallarino. Cartoon-obsessed monomaniac: that's what he'd been called once, in a letter to the editor, by a politician whose vanity he'd wounded. Now his eyes, always tired, gazed at the inhabitants of downtown Bogotá: the lottery-ticket seller resting on the stone wall; the student waiting for a bus, walking north and looking over his shoulder; the couple stopped in the middle of the sidewalk, man and woman, both office workers, both dressed in dark blue suits with white shirts, holding both of each other's hands but not looking at each other. All of them would react at the mention of his name—with admiration or repugnance, never with indifference—but none of them would be able to identify him. If he committed a crime, none of them could pick him out of a police lineup of usual suspects: *Yes, I'm sure, it's number five, the bearded one, the thin one, the bald one.* Mallarino, for them, didn't have particular features, and the few readers who'd met him over the years often commented with surprise: *I hadn't imagined you bald, or thin, or bearded.* His was the kind of baldness that didn't call attention to itself; when he met someone he'd seen only once before, Mallarino often received the same disconcerted commentaries: "Have you always looked like that?" Or: "How strange. I didn't notice when we met." Maybe it was his expression, which devoured people's attention the way a black hole devours light: his eyes with drooping lids looking out from behind his glasses with a sort of permanent sadness, or the beard that hid his face like an outlaw's bandana. His beard used to be black; it was still full, but had gone gray: slightly more at the chin and sideburns, slightly less on the sides of his face. It didn't matter: it kept him hidden. And Mallarino was still unrecognizable, an anonymous being on the teeming streets. That anonymity gave him a puerile pleasure (like a child hiding in forbidden rooms) and had calmed Magdalena, his wife back then. "In this country they kill people for less," she used to say to him when a general or drug baron came off badly in one of his drawings. "It's better that no one knows who you are or what you look like. It's better that you can go out and buy milk and I won't worry if you take your time."

His gaze swept over the twilight universe of the Parque Santander. It took just an instant to spot three people reading the paper, his paper, and he thought that all three would soon pass or had already passed their eyes over the letters of his name in print and then his signature, that clear uppercase letter that soon deteriorated into a chaos of curves and ended up disintegrating into a corner, the sad trail of a crashing plane. Everyone knew the space where his cartoon had always been: in the very center of the first page of opinion columns, that mythic place where Colombians go to hate their public figures or find out why they love them, that great collective couch of a persistently sick country. It was the first thing anyone's eyes saw when they reached those pages. The black square, the slender strokes, the line of text or brief dialogue beneath the frame: the scene that left his desk each day and was praised, admired, commented on, misinterpreted, later repudiated in a column of the same newspaper or another, in the irate letter of an irate reader, in a debate on some morning radio show. Yes, it was a terrible power. There was a time when Mallarino desired it more than anything else in the world; he worked hard to get it; he enjoyed it and exploited it conscientiously. And now, when he was sixty-five years of age, the very political class he'd so attacked and hounded and scorned from his redoubt, mocked without consideration or respect for the ties of family or friendship (and he'd lost quite a few friends as a result; even a few relatives no longer spoke to him), that very same political class had decided to put the gigantic Colombian machinery of sycophancy into action to create a public homage that, for the first time in history, and perhaps the last, would celebrate a cartoonist. "This is not going to happen again," Rodrigo Valencia, publisher of the newspaper for the last three decades, said to him when he called, diligent messenger, to tell him about the official visit Valencia had just received, the accolades he'd just heard, the intentions the organizers had just proposed. "It's an offer that's not going to be repeated. It would be silly to turn it down."

"Who said I was going to turn it down?" asked Mallarino.

"Nobody," said Valencia. "Well, I did. Because I know you, Javier. And so do they, truth be told. If not, why would they come here and ask me first?"

"Oh, I see. You're the negotiator. You're the one who'll convince me."

"More or less," said Valencia. His voice was guttural and deep, one of those voices that give orders naturally, or whose demands are accepted without a fuss. He knew it; he'd grown accustomed to choosing the words that best suited his voice. "They want to hold it in the Teatro Colón, Javier, imagine that. Don't let the chance slip by, don't be an idiot. Not for you, don't get me wrong, you don't matter to me. For the newspaper."

Mallarino let out a snort of annoyance. "Well, let me think about it," he said.

"For the newspaper," said Valencia.

"Call me tomorrow and we'll talk," said Mallarino. And then: "Would it be upstairs in the Foyer Hall?"

"No, Javier, this is what I'm trying to tell you. They're going to have it on the main stage."

"On the main stage?"

"That's what I'm telling you, man. This thing's serious."

They confirmed it later—Teatro Colón, main stage, the thing was serious—and the place seemed scarcely appropriate: there, under the fresco of the six muses, behind the curtain where Ruy Blas and Romeo and Othello and Juliet shared the same enchanted space, on the same stage where he'd witnessed so many beautiful artifices since he was a boy, from Marcel Marceau to *Life Is a Dream*, he was now getting ready to play an artifice of his own creation: the favored son, the honored citizen, the illustrious compatriot with lapels wide enough to hold as many medals as necessary. So he'd turned down the transportation the ministry had offered to put at his disposal: a bulletproof black Mercedes with darkened windows, according to the description over the phone from a tremulously voiced secretary, that would have picked him up at his house in the mountains and dropped him off on the stone steps of the theater, right below the wrought iron and glass canopy, a young damsel arriving at the ball where she would meet her prince. No, this afternoon Mallarino had come down to the city in his old Land Rover and left it in a parking lot at Fifth and Nineteenth. He wanted to arrive at his own apotheosis on foot, approach like everybody else, appear suddenly at a corner and feel that his mere presence might send a tremor through the air, spark conversations, turn heads; he wanted to announce, with this single gesture, that he hadn't lost a speck of his old independence: he still had the clout to make any of them a target, and that wasn't going to be changed by power or tributes or a bulletproof Mercedes with tinted windows. Now, on the bootblack's chair, while the brush moved over his shoes so quickly that it turned into a thick brown line, the way fans seem to no longer have blades as they spin into whirring white circles, Mallarino found himself asking a question that hadn't been in his head before he came into town: What would Rendón have done in his place? If what had happened to Mallarino had happened to Rendón, what would he have done? Would he have received the tribute with satisfaction, or would he have accepted it with resignation or cynicism? Would he have refused it? Ah, but Rendón had refused in his own way: on October 28, 1931, he went into La Gran Vía, ordered a beer, drew a sketch, and shot himself in the temple. In seventy-nine years, nobody had been able to explain why.

"That's three thousand five hundred, chief," the bootblack said. "Your Honor's got pretty big feet, you know."

"So I've been told," said Mallarino.

"All the better for me, you'll pardon my saying," said the man.

"That's for sure," said Mallarino. "Better for you."

Mallarino reached into his trouser pockets, the front and then the back, before moving to his gray raincoat, where his fingers found, tangled in a number of threads like fish in seaweed, a till receipt and a greenish wallet, worn with use and falling apart. "Here," he said to the bootblack with calculated generosity, "and keep the change." The man flattened out the note, took an old leather wallet out of his wooden crate, and tucked it inside, without folding it, sliding it in with precision. Then he raised his tired face, squeezed his eyes shut, opened them again: "Do you want to ask them, chief?"

"Ask what?"

"About the gentleman you were looking for. I can ask my colleagues, it's no trouble."

Mallarino didn't say no; he waved his hand in the air as if erasing the last words and stammered a thank you. But he liked the man, his natural courtesy, his good manners: endangered species in this inelegant, sour-faced, coarse Bogotá, hardly the South American Athens it used to flatter itself as being. Who had said that in Bogotá even the bootblacks quoted Proust? Must have been some Englishman, Mallarino said to himself; only an Englishman would be capable of such a pronouncement. Of course, it had been said some time ago: said in another city, the disappeared city, the phantom city, the city of Ricardo Rendón, the city of La Gran Vía, the entrance of which Mallarino could have seen, a few decades ago, from the spot on the sidewalk where he now lingered distractedly, a short step from the hostile roadway, his gaze lost between the short buses with their brightly lit windows. But the place had disappeared. Many shops and many cafés had disappeared, La Gran Vía among them. Had Rendón's ghost emerged from that phantom door? But it wasn't a ghost: someone dressed like Rendón, someone resembling Rendón, with the same wide-brimmed hat, with the same unruly bow tie: that was all. Maybe, thought Mallarino, it was the proximity to La Gran Vía or to its former location that had set off that vision, or maybe it was one of those false memories we all have. What a strange thing memory is, allowing us to remember what we have not experienced. Mallarino remembered Rendón strolling through the center of Bogotá, meeting León de Greiff in El Automático, arriving home, drunk and alone and sad, in the early hours. . . . Fictitious memories, invented memories. There was no reason to be surprised: it was impossible, on a day like today, to pretend that Rendón had no part in his thoughts. *The gentleman you were looking for.* No, he wasn't actually looking for him: rather, he was on his way to re-place him, to occupy his throne or inherit his scepter or whatever imbecilic metaphor, like the ones he'd read in two or three opinion columns by people as well informed as they were affected, as good at remembering as at brown-nosing. "It's a poor sort of memory that only works backwards": a free association had brought that phrase to mind. Where was it from, and to what was it referring? But then he stopped thinking of it, because he'd glanced again at his watch and the angle of the hands turned into a reproach: Was he going to arrive late even for his own coronation?

He began to walk against the flow of the crowd along Seventh Avenue, crossing Jiménez Avenue and the Plazo-leta del Rosario into La Candelaria, dodging street sellers determined to sell everything that can be sold—buy ciga-rettes, buy cheap gold, buy toy cars or polished emeralds, buy umbrellas or shoelaces, buy lollipops with chewing gum centers, chewing gum without lollipops, chocolate-covered raisins—and thinking that in downtown Bogotá one always has the sensation of walking against the flow, the afternoon crowds like a strong headwind. Determined to overcome the resistance, Mallarino lowered his head, raised his shoulders, and stuck his hands in the pockets of his raincoat, the unfathomable depths of which never ceased to surprise him. And that's what he was thinking about, the nooks of his raincoat he seemed not to have completely explored, when he heard the clicking of high heels behind him, or rather he realized he'd heard it when the heel-clicking ended with a hand on his shoulder, as delicate as a falling leaf, and he turned around, half surprised and half curious, to find the face of Magdalena, her hair so fair the gray ones blended in, her slender eyebrows arched, her ironic smile: the whole landscape of features Mallarino had once known the way he now knew the view from his window.

"I think we're going to the same place," she said.

There was no resentment in her voice: rather a kindness resembling something forgiven or perhaps forgotten (though Magdalena's voice had always been capable of all kinds of sorcery). Mallarino kissed her on the cheek and remembered her perfume, and something awoke in his chest. It was true, Magdalena's radio station was nearby. "I think you're right," he said. "If you want I'll walk you there." She smiled and took his arm, or linked her arm through Mallarino's, like she did when they were married and used to go for walks together in town, before they'd allowed life, headstrong life, to have its own way.

"Typical of you," she said, "to arrive on foot."

She'd noticed. Magdalena always noticed: she'd always

been that way. Her liquid eyes—today, for some reason, brighter than he remembered them—saw everything, took everything in.

"What do you expect," said Mallarino. "At our age, a person's not going to change."

When they got married, in a small-town church with limestone walls and cobbled steps leading into the square and where one could easily turn an ankle, Mallarino had been drawing cartoons for just under a year—two a month, with luck—for a newspaper with conservative tendencies and family capital, one of those publications that never become leaders in the field but seem to have always existed and whose editions aren't sold by the street vendors but show up in the drugstores and cafés when everyone's forgotten all about them. That minor job, Mallarino thought, with involuntary scorn, did not form a part of his great projects: if he'd dropped out of his architecture course before completing the second year, if he'd refused to use his father's contacts to get a job without a diploma in one of the important firms, it had been to pursue his true vocation, or to make the most of his virtuosity, for even his parents had to bow to the evidence of his talent on the afternoon the painter Alejandro Obregón—who at that time was painting his oils of doves in a third-floor apart-

ment at Twelfth Avenue and Seventeenth Street—visited
the family home, stood in front of a life-size nude Mallarino was drying with a portable hair-dryer, and exclaimed
a ten-word sentence that was like a bullfighter authorizing
a novice to take his place in the ring: "But how the hell did
this kid learn to paint?"

Painting was his thing. His future (the ghosts that appeared in his head when he pronounced this word) was on
canvas. So at that time the caricatures were a short-term
way of earning a living, getting by while large frames piled
up in the courtyard and the house filled with the smell of
turpentine and with canvases covered in female forms, all
more or less disguised versions of Magdalena, their colors
changing according to the mood of the light coming
through the windows. The newspaper paid him badly and
late, and only when it actually used one of his drawings:
it was not unusual for Mallarino to send five or six cartoons a week and receive them back at the end of the
month with a note typed by a secretary, on embossed
letterhead, in which the opinion page editor regretted in
too many words not being able to use Mallarino's work
this time. At the age of twenty-five, he did not yet know
that this was common practice in the country's newsrooms;
Magdalena didn't know either, but she was the one to sug-
gest sending just one cartoon and not sending another
until the first was published. "And if they don't publish

it?" asked Mallarino. "We'll just wait till they do," she said. "But the moment passes. Cartoons are like fish: if they're not used today, they can't be used tomorrow." "Well, that may well be the case," said Magdalena, concluding the subject. "But that's their problem."

And of course she was right. Subjected to rationing, the newspaper began to publish everything Mallarino sent, and even to increase the frequency of his appearances. For five months the situation was ideal. Then, in the month of August, the Colombian president and the Chilean president signed a joint declaration in which both countries officially expressed their respect for ideological diversity. Mallarino drew them both, the Colombian with his eternal involuntary smile and the Chilean with his thick-framed tinted glasses. *Look, my dear Salvador, in Colombia it doesn't matter if you're Liberal or Conservative,* read the first line of the text. And the second: *What matters is that you come from a good family.* The drawing was finished in one draft, and Mallarino left it at the front desk of the newspaper, well sealed inside a cardboard envelope, inside a plastic bag from the market (it had been drizzling). But the next day, when he opened the newspaper, he found that the second line of the text had disappeared, and its absence was like a crack in the earth, a drain down which everything seeps away. "I want someone to explain it," he

said that afternoon in the editorial office: he'd arrived by
taxi, because his urgency warranted it, with the newspaper
rolled up like a telescope and wrinkled in his sweaty fist.
He didn't want his voice to tremble; to prevent it, he tried
raising it, but the result was not good.

"There's nothing to explain," said the editor in chief.
He had a double chin and small eyes; among the dispro-
portioned features of his face, the mouth seemed to move
independently from the rest of his muscles. "Don't fly off
the handle, Javier, this happens all the time."

"To whom? Who does this happen to all the time?"

"To everyone who draws cartoons here. Hadn't you noticed? Everyone knows that sometimes things have to be
cut. Now you're going to tell me the editor doesn't have
that right."

"In a column," said Mallarino. It was a terrible defense,
but he couldn't think of another. "Not in a cartoon."

"In cartoons too, dear boy, don't be naive. Because they
also appear in the newspaper and they also take up space.
What am I supposed to say to the advertisers? Tell me,
what do I tell them?"

Mallarino said nothing.

"This is what I'm going to tell them," the editor went
on, starting to walk in circles, both thumbs firmly stuck in
his belt. "I'm going to tell them: Look, my good advertis-

ers, gentlemen who pay me thousands of pesos a year, I have a problem. I can't print your ads, in spite of the fact that the money you pay me is what pays the journalists' wages. And do you know why, gentlemen? Because a cartoonist doesn't like to have the space for his drawings trimmed by even a millimeter. That eventually we'll have to close the newspaper down doesn't matter, but the cartoon page cannot be touched. Geniuses are like that, my dear advertisers, be grateful you don't have to deal with any. That's what I'll tell them: that geniuses are like that. Would that do it, Mallarino?"

Mallarino said nothing.

"We'll stop paying our journalists. Or, if you like, we'll stop paying you. Fair enough?"

Mallarino said nothing.

"Look, go home and have a shot of *aguardiente*. And calm down: next time, someone will call young sir and ask his permission. So he won't have a tantrum, for crying out loud, which is tiring for all of us." He pointed to the interior window of his office, a huge fresco of faces pretending not to look, a constellation of sidelong glances: "Look at these people. As if this were a market square, how embarrassing."

And then Mallarino said his final words: "Would you give me back the original, please?"

He went out to find himself in a darkened city—the

low clouds, black suits of the passersby, and metallic whisper of umbrellas opening all around; a downpour soaked him before he had time to get home. Hair plastered to his scalp and shoulders hunched under the weight of the rain, he didn't seem to notice he'd turned into a high-plains scarecrow. *Next time*: the two words kept echoing in his head, ricocheting off the walls of his skull, when he recounted the whole episode to Magdalena. "Next time," she said, handing him a mauve towel as if handing him a declaration of war for his approval and signature. "Next time. Well, it seems to me like there isn't going to be any next time."

"What do you mean?" said Mallarino.

"Just what you heard," said Magdalena. "We'll tell them to go to hell, teach them a lesson."

Magdalena was a couple of years younger than him, but she went through life like an overseer strolling around a plantation. She possessed an intelligence as brutal as her obstinacy and was not hindered by the fact that her surname was that of the founder of a legendary legal firm— two carpeted floors of a building overlooking the Parque Nacional—although she'd always declared herself in rebellion against the surname, against her father, and against everyone's expectations: instead of enrolling in the faculty of law to carry on the family tradition, Magdalena had become one of the best-paid serial actresses on national radio, the voice that—from *Kalimán the Incredible* to *Arandú, Prince of the Jungle*—held the whole country spellbound at twelve noon. Those melodramas had been a natural step for her, a prolongation of the advertisements she'd read since adolescence, when publicity firms began vying for the privilege of hiring her voice. Magdalena's voice: husky and smooth at the same time, one of those voices that paralyze the hand of someone about to turn a dial, that translate the chaos of the world and convert its obscure jargon into a diaphanous tongue. "A cello that speaks," Mallarino called her, and now that voice was saying *We'll tell them to go to hell,* and Mallarino was thinking *Yes, to hell,* and he was also thinking *Teach them a lesson.* The most difficult times, in Mallarino's experience, were reduced to their simplest expression when Magdalena spoke of them, and that's what happened that afternoon: after the conversation, after the hot shower Mallarino took to warm up after getting chilled by the rain, after the improvised sex and the well-planned meal, everything was clear.

Magdalena took the plates and cutlery and colored sisal placemats to the kitchen while Mallarino brought a piece of paper, a quill pen, and a bottle of ink, which he placed in the center of the table, still warm from the heat of the serving dishes. In twenty minutes, while she put away the leftovers and meticulously covered the containers with sheets of tinfoil, he quickly drew a self-portrait and put it in the envelope with the drawing of the presidents. He had fun caricaturing himself for the first time: the premature baldness, the bushy black beard he'd inherited from his father, and the thick angular glasses, two little boxes of black acetate that did not manage to hide his wary eyes, his studiedly helpless gaze. Where his mouth would be, a gag straight out of the movies; beneath the drawing, the caption. *The oligarchy doesn't like to be talked about,* ran the first line. And then: *They wouldn't want us noticing that they're still right there.* In the envelope there was another document: a handwritten letter to Pedro León Valencia. He was the editor in chief of *El Independiente,* the oldest liberal newspaper in the country, and a man of strong convictions. "I'd like to offer you a package," wrote Mallarino in his own diploma writer's calligraphy, but with words dictated by Magdalena: "I'm sending one original cartoon, one censored cartoon, and one cartoon on censorship. If you can publish them all together, the package is yours; if not, return it and I'll look for another paper." Magdalena insisted on delivering the envelope, so Mallarino wouldn't appear needy (she never lost sight of these strategies of life in society), and that very evening their telephones began to ring in a hysterical chorus. It was the editor of the opinion page, a man Mallarino knew and had never liked: he was one of those professional victims incapable of delivering good news without disguising his envy. And Mallarino knew he was phoning to give him good news: he could sense it in the hostility of his tone, in his words with syllables cut off as if with a machete; Mallarino was surprised his rancor or envy didn't make the receiver splutter.

"The boss wants to offer you a permanent position," said the little man.

"But I don't want that," said Mallarino. "I don't want to be on anyone's staff."

"Don't be silly, Mallarino. A staff position is what every cartoonist dreams of. A guaranteed salary. Maybe you don't get it."

"I get it," said Mallarino. "But I don't want it. Pay me the same, but without being on the staff. I promise I won't draw for anyone else. And you people promise you'll publish what I send even if it's sometimes against your friends. Go ask your boss, and tell me."

It was a risky move, but it worked: the three drawings appeared the next day, and so, temporarily disguised as a comic strip, calling the reader so eloquently from the center spread, no longer the mere protest of a young man who fancies himself an artist, they became an elaborate narrative of media betrayal, a condemnation of censorship, and a noisy mocking of bourgeois vulnerability, all done by one of that bourgeoisie's most representative sons. "Your husband's gone mad," Magdalena's father told her. "Or maybe he's turned into a communist and nobody's noticed yet." She passed the message on to Mallarino, raising her left eyebrow and with a slightly crooked smile, a sign of evident satisfaction that, in the semi-darkness of their room, at the end of a day full of tensions and worries, was almost erotic. Mallarino turned on the radio, to see if he could find a repeat broadcast of the day's episode of *Kalimán*, but Magdalena, who detested hearing herself, covered her ears with histrionic gestures, and he found himself forced to look for something else. Magdalena found it impossible to recognize herself in the actual broadcast: that voice that wasn't her voice, she said; rather, there was a national conspiracy to wait for her to leave the studio and then rerecord, with another, better-trained actress, everything she had recorded. Mallarino held his arm out and Magdalena leaned her head on his chest, put her arms around him, and let out a couple of catlike noises he didn't manage to understand. After a few seconds of silence, Mallarino noticed that Magdalena's body changed weight—her forearm and her elbow, her clean-smelling head—and knew she'd fallen asleep. He found a football match on the radio, and before falling asleep as well, lulled by his wife's quiet snores and the monotonous usual story from the commentators, he heard Apolinar Pani-agua score twice for Millonarios and thought of something completely unrelated to those goals, but to do with the drawing in *El Independiente*: Mallarino thought that he couldn't prove it, that he couldn't have said how or why, but that his place in the world had just changed irrevocably.

He was not mistaken. That was the first day of the most intense period of his life, a decade in which he went from anonymity to having a reputation and then notoriety, all at the pace of one cartoon a day. His work was the metronome that regulated his life: just as others measured time by World Cups or film premieres, Mallarino associated every important event in his life with the cartoon he was working on at the time (the eyeless cheekbones of the guerrilla fighter Tirofijo, kidnapper of the Dutch consul, would always evoke his father's first bout of cancer; the aged and infirm Francisco Franco's goose neck and nonexistent chin, the birth of his daughter, Beatriz). His routine was unassailable. He got up a little before first light, and while he made the coffee he heard the whisper of two newspapers sliding halfway under the door, the doorman's judicious footsteps walking away, the machinery of the elevator—its regretful electronic grumble—coming back to life. He read the papers standing up at the kitchen counter, with the pages spread open over the surface, so he could mark the interesting subjects with a rough charcoal circle. When he finished, with the cold light of the Andean morning timidly filling the living room, he took the radio into the bathroom and listened to the news while giving his body over to the consecutive pleasures of shitting and showering, a ritual that cleansed his intestines, yes, but especially his head: he cleansed it of the muck accumulated the previous day, all the critiques trying to be intelligent that were nothing but resentful, all the opinions that should have seemed only idiotic but actually struck him as criminal, all the collisions with that strange country of brotherly hatred where mediocrity was rewarded and excellence penalized. In the shower, with the hot water flowing over his skin and producing delicate shivers of pores closing and opening up again, sometimes he couldn't even make out the words from the radio; but some mechanism of his imagination allowed him to guess or intuit them, and when he turned off the water and pushed open the sliding door—two or three extra movements, since the aluminum edge invariably stuck in its frame—it was as if he hadn't missed anything. Seconds later, leaving behind the bathroom world of steam, the day's image had been born in his head, and Mallarino had only to draw it.

It was, and would go on being for a long time, the happiest moment of the day: a half hour, or a whole one, or two, when nothing existed outside the friendly rectangle of card and the world that was being born within it, invented or cast by the lines and marks, by the to-and-fro of India ink. During those minutes Mallarino even forgot the indignation or irritation or mere rebellious instinct that had given rise to the drawing in the first place, and all his attention, just as happened in the middle of sex, concentrated on an attractive form—a pair of ears, an exaggerated set of teeth, a lock of hair, a deliberately ridiculous bow tie—outside of which nothing else existed. It was total abandonment, broken only when the drawing turned out to be difficult or stubborn: on those rare occasions Mallarino locked himself in the guest bathroom with a copy of *Playboy* in one hand, and some quick relief with the other left him ready to finish his battle with the drawing, always victoriously. In the end, he stood up, took a step back, and looked at the paper like a general overlooking a battle; then he signed it, and only then did the drawing begin to form part of the world of real things. By some useful spell, his cartoons were free of consequences while he was doing them, as if no one was ever going to see them, as if they existed for him alone, and only when he signed them did Mallarino realize what he'd just done or said. Then he put the card in an envelope, without staring intently at it—"like Perseus putting the Medusa's head in the silver bag," Mallarino would tell a journalist years later—and the envelope in a scruffy leather briefcase that Magdalena had bought him at a flea market; he took a bus to the newspaper offices, a sort of bunker where all the inhabitants, from the cleaning women to the photographers, seemed to be the color of concrete; he handed in the envelope and went back to his life without really knowing what to do with his hands, as if dispossessed. Why was he still doing what he did, what real effect would his cartoon have on the out-of-focus and remote world that began at the edge of his worktable, that slim wooden precipice? Was it disenchantment he was feeling, a sense of emptiness, or had he simply lost his bearings? Was he falling into the old trap of having more ire than ink? The world around him was changing: Pedro León Valencia, legendary publisher, had stepped aside in favor of his eldest son, and Mallarino recognized that part of the pleasure of working for *El Independiente* had been working with a legend, being the discovery or invention of a legend. Once the novelty of the early years started to wear off, having lost the egocentric urge to open the newspaper every morning and see his name in black-and-white, Mallarino was beginning to wonder if it had been worthwhile giving up his oils and canvases for this: the adrenaline rush he no longer felt, the imaginary reactions of imaginary readers he never got to meet, this vague and perhaps false sensation of public importance that caused him only private trouble; relatives who greeted him less warmly, friends who stopped inviting him to dinner with their wives. For what?

That's when he received, in a single prodigious day, the answer to all his questions. He'd acquired the habit of walking around downtown in the afternoons, buying his daughter absurd stickers for an absurd album Magdalena insisted she fill up, or getting his shoes shined and talking politics with the bootblacks, or simply watching life with a sort of hunger that demanded he stay out on the streets instead of returning to his morning seclusion, take off his jacket and feel his arms brush up against other arms and pick up the smell of living bodies, of the food they eat and the piss they leave in corners. That afternoon was a Tuesday, which was the day of the week Mallarino would go to the Avianca Building to collect his mail from his mailbox (the metallic gray, deep little box that brought him boundless pleasure, like a magician's hat does a child) and later sit in some nearby café to read his magazines and answer his letters. He arrived at Seventh Avenue by the National Library and from there, along the eastern sidewalk, began to walk south, sometimes noticing the noisy, disorderly, relentless city, sometimes so distracted that the building came into view almost unexpectedly, its long straight lines penetrating the sky and struck, on a sunny afternoon, by a dense light that seemed not of this world. As he went in, his hand would already be feeling for his keychain in his pocket and separating out the mailbox key so he wouldn't have to search for it in front of the cemetery wall of post boxes. And that's how it had gone that time: Mallarino made his way through the corridors (through their whitish light, which drew circles under everyone's eyes) and turned to the little gray door; he stretched out his arm and his precise hand, that hand that could draw exact ninety-degree angles without any instruments, and placed the tip of the key into the lock the way a medieval knight would have put the tip of his lance against his rival's chest. But the key did not go in.

He thought at first that he'd gone to the wrong box. He leaned down toward the little door and looked at the number on the metal tag with all its digits, the same as ever, the ones Mallarino knew by heart. He hadn't gotten it wrong. The revelation arrived late, like a careless guest: there was a shadow or texture that made him look more closely at the metallic surface, and only when he was inches away from the lock did he realize it had been blocked up with chewing gum. It was a hardened paste (it must have been there several days) that filled the slot without overflowing the edges: a conscientious piece of work. Mallarino touched the paste with the tip of the key, probed, pushed, scratched a little, tried a carving movement with his wrist, but got nowhere: the dried gum paste remained firm. "Hey, what a nasty trick to play on someone," said a voice, and Mallarino turned his head to find a gold tooth glinting in the middle of an unshaven face. "No way to fix that, huh? People have no respect these days." And Mallarino soon found himself climbing a mottled stairway, walking till he reached a counter, handing over his ID, and watching as a petite woman went through books, opened drawers and closed them again, produced a photocopy of a form from somewhere and asked if Mallarino would be paying in cash or by check, turned a deaf ear when Mallarino protested and said he hadn't lost the key, that someone had put chewing gum in the lock, and the woman told him it was all the same to her, and how was he paying: cash or check? Then there were stamps in purple ink, carbon paper and pastel-colored receipts, time wasted in a hard and hostile plastic chair, and, finally, a shout ringing against the concrete walls: "Mallarino? Javier Mallarino?"

A skinny, grief-stricken locksmith—his overalls smelling of improperly dried clothes—went back with him to face the rebellious mailbox, took a series of unnameable tools from his leather belt, the metals giving off sparks under the neon lights, and what followed was the violation of the lock, or what Mallarino perceived as a violation, a violent and treacherous penetration of his private life, in spite of the fact that he'd given his authorization and consent, in spite of his being present during the whole process. He felt something like physical pain at the breaking of the lock, at the snap of the little door; he was saddened by the vulnerability of his collection of magazines looking at him imploringly from the shadowy depths: the latest *Alternativa*, the latest *New Yorker*, a back issue of *Le Canard Enchaîné* a Parisian colleague had sent him. He wanted to leave and be home already, in his refuge, reading with a glass of beer, hearing or sensing the reassuring presence of his wife and daughter. But he still had to witness the installation of the new lock and get the new keys and sign more papers and put tips in faceless hands before going back out onto Seventh Avenue carrying his leather bag slung across his chest, the back of his neck sweaty, his eyes tired from so much darkness. Later he would think it had all begun with that tiredness, or the disorientation that always overwhelmed him after contending with the senseless bureaucracy of this country, or simply the white color of the envelope, that immaculate white, with no address or writing of any kind, no stamps, no blue and red stripes that revealed a letter's having arrived from abroad. He'd started taking the magazines out of his bag (impatient to begin leafing through them) and had his hand stuck inside it, fingers moving as if through a card catalog, head looking down to see the covers, when he noticed the corner sticking out between the pages. He stopped in the middle of the square, looked at the front and back of the envelope, then opened it. "Javier Mallarino," read the typed text of the letter, with neither date nor address. "With your warping of the truth you have assaulted and discredited the Armed Forces of our Republic, playing into the hands of the enemy, you are an UNPATRIOTIC LIAR and we hereby notify you that the patience of those who are LOYAL to our beloved country is wearing thin, we know where you live and where your daughter goes to school, we will not hesitate to punish with the harshest severity any further infringements against our honor." On the last line, over to the right, with no *Regards*, no *Sincerely*, no *Yours faithfully*, a single word that seemed to be shouting from the page: "PATRIOTS."

The first thing he did when he got home was to show Magdalena the letter, and he knew she was genuinely worried when she started making fun of the wording and grammar. Between the two of them they tried to remember the last cartoon he'd drawn on a military subject; they had to go back several weeks to a series of three drawings in which a disconsolate horse was talking to a woman who was handling some iron structures. Malla-

rino had drawn those scenes after Feliza Bursztyn, a Bogotá sculptor famous for working with scrap iron, had
been accused of subversive activities, imprisoned in the
army's stables, manhandled and humiliated, and later
forced into exile. Magdalena and Mallarino propped the
originals up on the long living room sofa and spent a
good while looking at them, as if wishing they could van-
ish from the recent past. That night they were so fright-
ened that they dragged a mattress into their bedroom so
Beatriz, who had just turned six, could go to bed there,
and the family slept like that, heaped up in the insuffi-
cient space, breathing stale air all night with their pressed-
wood door securely locked. Days of paranoia would
follow, Mallarino looking over his shoulder on the city's
streets and returning home before dark, but later, when
the memory of the threat began to fade away, what they'd
remember would be the reaction of Rodrigo Valencia,
who'd burst out laughing on the other end of the phone
line when Magdalena called him at the newspaper, the
day after Mallarino received the note, to tell him what
had happened. Mallarino watched Magdalena furrow her
brow, the telephone stuck to her ear, then heard her faithfully relay the message:

"Rodrigo says congratulations, you've finally made it.
He says you're nobody in this country until somebody
wants to hurt you."

On the left-hand side of the stage, hidden in the wing between backdrops, Mallarino was waiting. The organizers of the tribute had asked him not to move from the spot until he was announced, and, obediently, he amused himself by looking at the velvet curtains and the grain of the wooden floorboards, but also by watching the hustle and bustle of people walking without tripping over the beams, the mysterious cables, the abandoned props like remains from old battles. The Teatro Colón was immersed in semidarkness. The audience, that audience who'd come to see him, had their eyes fixed on the back of the stage, on the images projected on a white screen while the voice of a professional announcer recounted Mallarino's biography over rather cheesy background music. Mallarino tried to peek out without being seen. The impossible angle didn't prevent him from recognizing himself painting in his parents' courtyard, or speaking to President Betancur, or opening the door to some cameramen who were making a documentary in his house up in the mountains, or posing beside an old drawing on the day of his first retrospective exhibition, at the beginning of the nineties. It was a caricature of Mikhail Gorbachev; Mallarino remembered it as if he'd drawn it yesterday: the classic bald head, and on it, instead of the by then famous birthmark, maps of Nicaragua and Iran. Behind Gorbachev, a worried and pensive Ronald Reagan asked: "Mikhail, are you saying I ran contraband?" "No, Ronald," Gorbachev answers. "I'm saying you're with the Iran-Contra band." The whole drawing had taken him just over an hour, but the easy joke in the text had always left him dissatisfied, and now Mallarino relived that dissatisfaction and wrote new drafts in his head, different combinations of the same words, less obvious puns. He was busy with that when he heard himself announced, and he had to go onstage, suffer the assault of the lights, feel the explosion of applause like a gust of wind and hear its uproar like a deluge.

Mallarino raised a hand by way of greeting; his mouth moved imperceptibly. He saw his vacant seat as if it were in fog; he saw faces greeting him, attentive hands outstretched to shake his and then go back to applauding, quick like those of a bootblack brushing shoes. Out of habit—but where did it come from, when had it started?—he took two pens and his note-taking pencil out of his pocket and placed them on the table in front of him, three perfectly parallel lines. The theater was full: in a flash he remembered previous visits, and in his head a Les Luthiers concert got mixed up with a zarzuela that he'd enjoyed a lot even though Luisa Fernanda, no less, had hit a false note in the first song. He looked for the box he'd sat in then, fourth to the right of the presidential, and found it occu-

pied by a group of six young people on their feet, applauding. Only when the rest of the audience began to sit down,
gradually, making delicate little waves on the sea of the
orchestra section, did he realize that the entire audience
had been standing until a moment before: they'd welcomed him to the stage with a standing ovation. In the
front row was Rodrigo Valencia, hands clasped over his
belly, elbows invading the seats next to him: Valencia always gave the impression that chairs were too small for
him. A voice came through the speakers. Mallarino had
to look around for its source, first at the table, then at the
cheap wooden lectern bearing the Colombian coat of
arms. Behind the lectern, the minister—Mallarino had
seen her on the news and had read her declarations: her
intentions were as laudable as her ignorance was vast—
began to speak.

"Were I to be asked what ex-President Pastrana looks
like," she said, "just as if I were asked what Franco or Ara-
fat looked like, the image that forms in my head is not a
photograph but a drawing by Maestro Mallarino. My idea
of many people is what he has drawn, not what I have
seen. It's possible, no, it's certain, that the same thing happens to many people here tonight." Mallarino listened to
her with his gaze glued to the table, feeling people's gazes
on him like a hand, fidgeting with a nonexistent ring: the
ring that was once on his left ring finger and that Malla-

rino still felt, the way amputees feel a missing limb. "In some way," the minister went on, "to be caricatured by Javier Mallarino is to have a political life. The politician who disappears from his drawings no longer exists. They go on to a better life. I've known many who have even told me: Life after Mallarino is much better." The witticism was rewarded with a brief ripple of laughter. So the little lady has a sense of humor, thought Mallarino, looking up; and in that instant, just as we will spot our own name lost in the middle of any page, Mallarino found Magdalena's luminous face in the middle of the smiling multitude. She was smiling too, but hers was a melancholy smile, the smile of things lost. What was going on in her life? They hadn't talked seriously for many years: they had agreed, with the solemnity of an international treaty, that mutual revelations about their private lives would serve only to complicate everything: to accelerate, like a bacteria, the decomposition of good memories, and to embitter Beatriz, whose adolescence had been a painstaking martyrdom in which she felt guilty about every one of the family's misfortunes, and the rest of her life had been a stubborn, speedy, headlong escape. For Mallarino, his daughter's life choices—her Catholic, provincial husband, her career with Médecins Sans Frontières—were nothing but a sophisticated way to escape from her family, from that surname that always touched off embarrassing reactions but also the painful experience of growing up as the daughter of a failed or broken couple. The only blemish on this night was the absence of Beatriz, who just that week had been obliged to make an unexpected trip to La Paz; in a few days she'd be on a longer, more planned one to an unpronounceable village in Afghanistan, and between the two she'd drop by to see him, or call so they could meet for lunch, and Mallarino knew, after that visit or that lunch, a desert of months and months without seeing her again would open before him. The minister was suddenly talking about Greek glasses and essential strokes, pronouncing words like *symbol*, like *allegory* and *attribute*, and Mallarino was remembering in the meantime a journalism seminar on editorial and opinion pages—with a pompous title and grandiloquent guest speakers—where he had been asked what he would change about his life and all he could think of was his relationship with Beatriz.

"With the passage of time, over the forty years we're here to celebrate today," the minister was saying meanwhile, "the great Mallarino's drawings have been getting sadder. His characters have hardened. His gaze has become more intransigent, more critical. And his cartoons, in general, have become more indispensable. I can't imagine a life without Javier Mallarino's daily cartoon, but nor can I imagine a country that could give itself the luxury of not having him." This, Mallarino admitted, had come out nicely: I wonder who writes her speeches. "And so today we are paying him this homage, a tiny recognition of an artist who has turned into the country's critical conscience. Today we present him with this medal, the highest honor our nation confers, but we present him with something else too, Maestro: we have a little surprise for you." Behind the table, at the back of the stage, the white screen appeared again, and illuminated on it was an image: it was the caricature of himself that Mallarino had drawn forty years earlier, that ironic self-portrait he'd used to defend himself from being censored and to begin his career at *El Independiente*. But there, on the screen, the image had a serrated frame, and above Mallarino's bearded face, at the level of his glasses, there was a price. It was a stamp. "Maestro Mallarino," said the minister, "allow me to present you with the first day cover of the national post office's new stamp, so that from now on letters mailed in our cities will also be an homage to your life and work." Mallarino saw the long hair spilling over her shoulders, the chest rising with nervous breaths, the hand that unleashed a jangle of bracelets as she handed him a black frame. From old habit, Mallarino identified the wood of the frame, the frosted glass, and the foam-core board. In the center of an enormous black space, deep as the night sky, was the stamp.

The frame changed hands and the deluge of applause burst out for a second time. Mallarino noticed a slight tickle at the nape of his neck and in the pit of his stomach. As he approached the lectern with the Colombian coat of arms, the flanks of which stuck out from behind like a bat's ears, he realized he was moved.

"Forty years," he said, leaning down toward the microphone, which suddenly looked like a fly's compound eye. "Forty years and more than ten thousand cartoons. And let me confess something to you all: I still don't understand anything. Or perhaps things haven't changed so much. In these forty years, it occurs to me now, there are at least two things that haven't changed: first, what worries us; second, what makes us laugh. That's still the same, it's still the same as it was forty years ago, and I'm very much afraid that it'll still be the same forty years from now. Good cartoons have a special relationship with time, with our time. Good cartoons seek and find the constant in a person: something that never changes, what stays the same and allows us to recognize someone we haven't seen in a thousand years. Even if a thousand years go by, Tony Blair will still have big ears and Julio César Turbay will still wear a bow tie. They're characteristics a person is grateful for. When a new politician has one of those characteristics, one immediately thinks: Please let him do something, let him do something so I can use it, so that feature won't be lost to the world's memory. One thinks: Please, don't let him be honest, don't let him be prudent, don't let him be a good politician, because then I won't be able to use him so frequently." A whisper of laughter could be heard, thin like the sound before a scandal. "Of course, there are politicians without distinctive features: absent faces. They're the most difficult, because they have to be invented, and so I do them a favor: they have no personality, and I give them one. They should be grateful. I don't know why, but they almost never are." Sudden guffaws bubbled up around the theater. Mallarino waited until the auditorium returned to respectful silence again. "No, they almost never are. But one has to get the idea out of one's head that it might matter. Great caricaturists don't expect applause from anyone, and that's not what they draw for: they draw to annoy, to embarrass, to be insulted. I have been insulted, I've been threatened, I've been declared persona non grata, I've been denied entry to restaurants, I've been excommunicated. And the only thing I always say, my only response to the complaints and aggression, is this: Caricatures might exaggerate reality, but they can't invent it. They can distort, but never lie." Mallarino paused theatrically, awaited applause, and the applause arrived. He raised his eyes then, looked up at the gods, and remembered having sat up there, at eighteen, the first time he brought a date to the Colón (a production of Verdi's *Un ballo in maschera*), and then looked back at the orchestra, searching for Magdalena, wanting to see the admiration on her face that he'd seen from time to time, that unconditional admiration that had once been his nourishment and objective. But his gaze fluttered around in space like a moth.

"Don't ever die, Mallarino!" shouted a woman's voice from somewhere in the front rows, possibly to his left, and Mallarino came out of his reverie. The voice that shouted was a mature voice, worn perhaps by cigarettes, perhaps by a lifetime of shouting out in theaters, and her peremptory tone was immediately celebrated by the audience with loud laughter. "Never!" shouted someone at the back. Mallarino feared for a second that the tribute was going to turn into a political rally. "Ricardo Rendón, my master," he hurried to say, "once compared the caricature to a stinger, but dipped in honey. I have that phrase mounted above my desk, more or less the way a sailor has a compass. *A stinger dipped in honey.* The identity of the caricaturist depends on the measures he uses of the two ingredients, but both ingredients always have to be there. There are no political cartoons that don't sting, and none without honey. There's no caricature if there's no subversion, because every memorable image of a politician is by nature subversive: it throws the solemn man off balance and reveals the impostor. But there's no caricature, either, if it doesn't bring a smile, even if it's a bitter smile, to the reader's face. . . ." Mallarino was saying this when his marooned gaze found Magdalena's eyes, with those slender eyebrows that arched like that, the way they were arched now, only when Magdalena was really paying attention: she was one of those women who could not feign interest, not even flirtatiously. A sudden urgency invaded him, a brutal desire to get down off the stage and be with her, to hear that voice that wasn't of this world, to speak in whispers with the past. Mallarino furrowed his brow (again the buffoon, he thought, again playing a part) and leaned in close to the microphone. "I would like to finish off," he said, "by remembering a certainty we often forget: Life is the best caricaturist. Life turns us into caricatures of ourselves. You have, we all have, the obligation to make the best caricature possible, to camouflage what we don't like and exalt what we like best. You'll understand that I'm not just talking about physical attributes, but of the mysterious traces life leaves on our features, the moral landscape, if you will—that's the only thing to call it—that moral landscape that gets drawn on our face as life goes by, as we go along making mistakes or getting things right, as we wound others or strive not to, as we lie or deceive or persist, sometimes at the cost of great sacrifices, in the ever difficult task of telling the truth. Many thanks."

The newspapers on the following day contained a litany of hackneyed praise. APOTHEOSIS IN THE COLÓN, was *El Tiempo*'s headline in the culture section, and *El Espectador* kept the matter on the front page: JAVIER MALLARINO GOES DOWN IN HISTORY, it read, the words floating over a grainy black-and-white photo with sharp contrasts, taken from a low angle by a good student of Orson Welles. That's what Mallarino said: "A good student of Orson Welles." Magdalena, whose face was emerging unhurriedly from sleep, the delicate muscles moving and settling in her forehead and her cheeks and her grin, all filling up with expression as a clay mask takes shape as it dries, looked at the image of Mallarino speaking behind the lectern with his arms open toward the theater and gave her opinion that if the photographer was thinking of *Citizen Kane*, the subject was thinking of *Titanic*. Leaning back on a disorderly pile of pillows, Mallarino could only wonder how they had ended up here, in his house in the mountains, waking up together, naked in the same bed, as they hadn't done for several lifetimes, each keeping a careful silence: not the habitual, daily silence, but the apprehensive silence people keep in order not to break—with clumsiness, with an inopportune question, with a sarcastic comment—the fragile equilibrium of reunions. Was this a reunion? The word was heavy on the tongue, like a flavor stuck there from the last meal: no, they mustn't talk about what had happened, mustn't commit that beginners' error. They talked about other things: her work at the university radio station, the musical program she'd been producing and presenting for the last few years, so agreeable because she never had to fight with any living people, with their vanities and pretensions. Magdalena recorded her program in a small studio with ochre walls, and in that fictitious solitude (because on the other side of the glass was the sound technician, and behind the technician, the noise of the world) she read the text that she herself, often with the help of those who knew more, had written. The stories of the songs, that's what Magdalena's program was about: telling people who Jude and Michelle were, what misfortunes lay behind *L'aigle noir*, what marital breakdown was referred to in *Graceland*. All this she told him now with her mouth hidden under the white duvet, protecting herself from the morning cold. It was cold, the house in the mountains: it would have been a scientific inaccuracy to say it was on the highland plateau, but it was close; if you went out for a walk, tall trees gradually disappeared and it wasn't impossible to run into some *frailejón* plants. Mallarino also liked the idea of living up at those altitudes and frequently used it to impress the gullible, even if it was an exaggeration: *my house in the Bogotá highlands*. He lifted the duvet to take a peek at Magdalena's body, and she slapped it down, making a tiny feather fly through the air.

"Don't start," she said, "I've got to get going."

It was all strange: it was strange, in the first place, that Magdalena recognized how strange it all was, that she understood in the same way, or seemed to understand; and the weight of her body in this bed was also strange, different from other bodies and curiously her own; and the familiarity was strange, the insolent familiarity they felt in spite of so many years of not being together; and, in particular, Mallarino's capacity to anticipate Magdalena's movements was very strange. "I've got a terrible day ahead of me," she said, "but let's see each other tomorrow, shall we? I'll take you out to lunch in town, so you don't get out of the habit." "Not in town," said Mallarino. "It makes our eyes water, us mountain folk." "What a weakling," said Magdalena. "A little pollution never hurt anybody." And then: "Will you come and pick me up at the station?" And then: "Let's say one o'clock." Mallarino said okay, they'd have lunch in town tomorrow, that he'd pick her up at one at the station, that a little pollution never hurt anybody, and at the same time he was making private predictions: now she'd roll over, turning her back on him, looking nowhere, and now she'd get out of bed in a single agile movement, slipping out without even pausing to sit on the edge

and stretch, and now she'd walk toward the bathroom
without looking back, or rather allowing herself to be
looked at, sure that Mallarino would be looking at her
the way he was looking at her, comparing her body with
the one he'd known years before and seeing the stretch
marks on her hips and shadows on her buttocks and being
jealous of them, because the stretch marks and shadows
weren't stretch marks and shadows but messengers of all
that had happened in his absence: all that Mallarino had
missed. The night before had been like making love with
a memory, with the memory of a woman and not with the
woman who was present, the way we keep feeling, after
stepping barefoot on a stone, the shape of the stone in the
arch of our foot. That's what Magdalena was: a sharp re-
minder. He saw her close the bathroom door and knew
(an uncomfortable, as well as so satisfactory, knowledge)
that he wouldn't see her come out again for a good quarter
of an hour. And finding himself there, in front of a picture
window looking out into the cloud forest, surrounded by
papers filled with news of his triumph and waiting for his
regained wife to come back to him, Mallarino felt a rare
calm. He wondered if this was what happy people felt, and
he was sure that it was when, a few hours later, after Magdalena had said good-bye with a kiss on the lips and he
had been working on the next cartoon, when the dogs

barked and the doorbell buzzed and Mallarino found himself with the young journalist from the previous evening who had asked him for an interview for some blog he'd never heard of, showing her into the living room and offering her something to drink, he noticed, not without surprise, that he had not the slightest intention of seducing her.

Her name was Samanta Leal. During the cocktail party the previous evening in the bar of the Teatro Colón to toast Mallarino and his award, she had approached, one of dozens, to ask him to autograph a copy of his most recent book. She brought it over still sealed in the unpleasant plastic Colombian books come in, which seems designed to discourage the reader and humiliate the author who, like Mallarino, tries to open the book to write an inscription. Mallarino, his fingers wet from the condensation on his whiskey glass, failed spectacularly at the task; when the interested party took the book in both hands and held it to her mouth and bit a corner of the plastic, Mallarino noticed the long fingers without any rings and then the parted lips and then the teeth that bit and then the whole mouth, which got into trouble with the bitten-off corner of plastic and tried to spit it out politely with comical movements of a very pink tongue (a little girl's tongue, Mallarino thought). It must have been the emotion of the moment, but it all seemed so sensual to him, so *concrete*, that he focused especially on the young woman's name as he wrote it. "For Samanta Leal," he said, pronouncing both the *l*'s carefully, as if to retain them, as if they were going to escape. "What do you want me to put?" "I don't know," she said, "put whatever you want." And he wrote: *For Samanta Leal, whatever you want.* None of what would happen with Magdalena had begun yet—she had congratulated him affectionately, but then she'd sat down on a red velvet chair and was laughing her head off with a writer from the coast—and Mallarino felt free to fantasize about an attractive thirty-something and to act on those fantasies. She read the inscription; instead of thanking him and taking her leave, she pursed her lips in a way that made Mallarino think of a freshly washed strawberry. "Well, what I want," Samanta Leal said, taking him by surprise, "is an interview." She mumbled the name of the site, an ugly English word full of consonants, and he said he knew nothing about blogs, that he didn't like them and didn't read them, and didn't really trust them. If in spite of all that she was still interested, he would expect her at his house tomorrow, at three o'clock sharp, so she could get what she could in forty-five minutes and then leave him free to get back to work.

And now here was Samanta Leal. She was wearing

green woolen tights, a gray skirt that didn't reach her knees, and a white blouse as smooth as a Malevich canvas, its only adornment the change of tone where her bra began. The eyes that had been dark the previous night, beneath the soft lights of the bar, were now green, and they opened wide to scrutinize the walls with that mixture of enchantment and disappointment with which we observe the places of those we admire. There was something impatient in her way of sitting down and crossing her legs, a certain restlessness, an uncomfortable electricity, and when she started asking random questions (How long had he lived in this house? Why had he decided to leave Bogotá?), Mallarino thought the same thing he'd thought before: that the interview was a pretext. Over time he'd learned to recognize the double intentions of those who approached him: the interview, the inscription, the brief conversation—they were just strategies serving a very different purpose: a job recommendation, the favor of leaving a particular politician alone, sex. He amused himself (though it was a dismayed amusement) by making private bets about Samanta Leal and the outcome of this visit, be it varying degrees of nudity or embarrassment. As the young woman asked questions, the disorder, the absence of method, was not the only feature that seemed duplicitous: in the calm of his house in the mountains, Samanta Leal's accent revealed unusual music to Mallarino that hadn't been noticeable the night before. She looked at the walls and he looked at her looking, seeing his own house through those surprised eyes, discovering, at the same time as she discovered, Débora Arango's toads wearing clothes, the *Cuadro rojo* by Santiago Cárdenas, or an Ariza landscape, somewhere between Boyacá and Japan. He watched her, looking for emotion or surprise on her face, but saw none: Samanta Leal looked over the paintings as if seeing an absence, as if what she was really looking for was missing among them.

"It was in 1982," said Mallarino. "I got tired of Bogotá, that's all, I got tired of a lot of things. I bought this house and two dogs, two German shepherds, a male and a female, whose puppies are the ones I have now. The ones with stars on their foreheads, all identical. Of course not all of them: I kept two and sold the rest, they eat as much as twenty people and mine are as big as horses, I don't know if you saw them." Samanta Leal said yes, she'd seen them and they'd scared her a little, to tell the truth. "No, they're not scary," said Mallarino. "Don't put this in the interview, but my dogs are the most cowardly creatures on earth: they're no good at guarding anything." And Samanta: "I won't. I promise. Nineteen eighty-two, you said?" And Mallarino: "Yes, that's right. Nineteen eighty-two, around the middle of the year. It's cold, but I like the cold. The plateau begins near here, you know. A little bit higher up the mountain and there it starts."

Samanta had taken three things out of her aquamarine handbag: a dull aluminum lighter, a pocket notebook, and a pen the same color as the handbag. She set the lighter on the table, and Mallarino realized it wasn't a lighter but rather a tiny digital recorder. He made some comment about it—"In my day people just took notes," perhaps, or perhaps "Journalists don't trust their own memories anymore"—and Samanta asked him how he got along with the new technologies, if he had become accustomed to using digital aids. "Never," said Mallarino. "I don't like them. I don't even make digital corrections, which is something many do. I don't. I draw by hand, and what comes out is what goes out. Digital technologies make everything boring, predictable, monotonous. One can get bored with this trade, señorita, and you have to invent tricks so that doesn't happen. For example, I sometimes challenge myself to draw an entire caricature without lifting my hand off the paper, or to draw in the background, behind the main scene, a miniature reproduction of a masterpiece. People don't stop to wonder why behind Hugo Chávez there might be a Rembrandt or a Raphael. . . . So, no, don't ask me about technology. It's not for me."

"And for sending them?"

"What about sending them?"

"Don't you use a computer?"

"I don't have a computer. I don't use the Internet, I

don't have e-mail. Didn't you know? I'm famous for that: absurdly famous, if you want my opinion. I don't know what's so strange about this. I have six or seven magazine subscriptions in three languages: tons of paper I never finish reading. With that and the television I have enough to keep me informed. I have cable, it's true, I have more news channels than I need, and I can even press pause to see someone's face better."

"But then how do you send them? How do you send the cartoons?"

"At first I used to take them in personally, of course. Then I started to use a fax machine—I used it for years. I still use it to communicate with people. That machine is my personal mail: if you want to write to me, you can do so by fax, and I'll answer you by fax. It's quite simple. But I used to use it to send in my cartoons. It didn't work. It broke up my lines, you know? Worried friends used to call: 'Are you ill? Is something wrong? Your lines aren't steady.' That's when they started to pick them up."

"Who?"

"The newspaper sends a courier. They've always had a courier driving around the city picking up and dropping off papers—it's called La Chiva. And when they come to collect my drawing, they call it La Chiva de Mallarino."

"But you live far away," said Samanta. "They'd have to cross the entire city. They come as far as this?"

"They're very kind," said Mallarino.

"They spoil you."

"I suppose so."

"It must be that you're important," said Samanta with a smile.

"Must be."

"And how does it feel?"

"How does what feel?"

"Being important. Being a country's conscience."

"Look," said Mallarino, "we live in confusing times. Our leaders aren't leading anything, much less telling us what's going on. That's where I come in. I tell people what's going on. The important thing in our society is not what goes on, but who tells us what's going on. Are we going to allow ourselves to be told only by politicians? That would be suicide, national suicide. No, we can't rely on them, we can't be satisfied with their version. We need to look for another version, from other people with other interests: from humanists. That's what I am: a humanist. I'm not a graphic jokester. I'm not a cartoon sketcher. I am a satirical illustrator. It has its risks as well, of course. The risk of turning into a social analgesic: the things I draw become more comprehensible, more easily assimilated. It hurts us less to confront them. I don't want my drawings to do that, of course I don't. But I'm not sure it can be avoided."

Samanta took the dictation diligently. Mallarino watched her copying it down in her notebook and reading over what she'd written with her big eyes even beneath the roof of her serious brow. "Could we go to your studio?" she asked, and Mallarino nodded. He pointed toward a darkened corridor and, at the end of the corridor, some steps of polished wood; he let her go ahead of him, in part out of chivalry, in part to observe the shape of her body through her skirt as she started up the steps. Mallarino had given many interviews lately, but this time, for some reason, was different: this time he wanted to talk. He felt loquacious, communicative, open and prepared to reveal himself. Perhaps it was the recent impression of his night with Magdalena, or perhaps the notion that his life, from this morning on, was a different life, but suddenly he started telling anecdotes, to do what he never did: talk about himself. He spoke of the day a mayor had changed his mind after a drawing was finished, and Mallarino resolved the matter by drawing another speech bubble with three short words: *Or maybe not.* He spoke of the businessman who once called him to ask him to stop drawing him the way he used to look now that he'd bought new glasses and had his protruding teeth fixed, but Mallarino kept drawing him the same way: Wasn't it unfair? "One time nothing occurred to me," said Mallarino. "It's unusual, but it happens. I drew myself with a cup of coffee, a blank piece of paper, and a thought bubble with the lightbulb of ideas completely dark. I sent the editor a note saying: 'Look, nothing has occurred to me. I have to submit the cartoon and not a single idea has occurred to me. I'm sorry. You decide whether to publish it or not.' The cartoon was published. The next day I began to receive congratulatory calls. Everybody was congratulating me. It turned out the day before there was a massive power outage in one of the poorest neighborhoods of Medellín. The cartoon was interpreted as criticizing the indolence of the administration, et cetera. I never told them the truth."

They had arrived at the studio. The afternoon light entered through the window that overlooked the city, that light smeared with mist, with dirty smoke, as if arriving tired from the other side of the plain. "The center of creation," said Samanta, stopping in the middle of the room, right below the skylight shedding that now scant light on top of her, and spinning around, sad lost caryatid, to devour with her eyes the filing cabinet, gray and metal and noisy, that kept watch over the room from one corner, and then the shelf of instruments, the hydraulic chair, and the worktable, a large wooden board, set at an exact twenty-two-degree angle, that leaned like a ramp to mount a cork wall, or so that the cork wall could send down, like toboggans, newspaper clippings, sketches, to-do lists, and photos of current public figures, victims (mostly) or beneficiaries of his caricatures. "Can you turn on the light?" asked Samanta. "It's hard to see." Obliging (but why, why so enthusiastic?), Mallarino flipped the switch; two halogen lamps came on in the ceiling and a wall covered in frames appeared out of nowhere. "It's my altar," said Mallarino. "I work facing the cork wall: that's my daily task, what I'm working on at the moment. But when things get annoying, when I start to ask myself why I got into this, or when reality gets so filthy it doesn't deserve to be drawn . . . then I come and stand over here, in front of this wall. A couple of minutes, that's enough. It's like confession for a Catholic, I imagine. All these are my personal priests, the ones who hear me, who give me advice. Do you want me to explain?"

But she didn't answer. "Do you want me to tell you about this wall, señorita?" Mallarino insisted, but Samanta had stopped looking at him, stopped taking notes, and her expression was no longer diligent and attentive; she'd suddenly acquired a concentrated and at the same time empty expression, like a crazy person.

"Ah, yes," he heard her say to no one, "here it is."

Five little words, or four words and an interjection: nobody would have believed them capable of inaugurating such a long night. Twenty-four hours later, remembering that precise instant, he would admire the composure with which Samanta walked over to the wall to take a closer look at one of the illustrations, as if she was discovering a new caricaturist instead of leaning over the precipice of her misfortune. Mallarino now knew that he was not going to tell her about Ricardo Rendón or discuss the stinger coated in honey, that he wouldn't explain the James Gillray drawing of Napoleon cutting a Europe-size slice from the globe, that he wouldn't show her Leonardo's grotesque heads, nor would he mention Della Porta or Lavater, for whom the character of a man could be found in the structure of his face. He knew, knew with total conviction, when he saw her turn around there, in front of the image of King Louis Philippe as Daumier had drawn him in 1834. Three distinct faces miraculously fit upon that pear-shaped head: one young and content, another pale and bitter, another sad and in shadow. The combination was grotesque, something no one would want to meet by surprise in the middle of the night. And instead of asking about the caricaturist or the caricatured one, instead of accepting explanations about the shape of the head or the triple expression on the face, Samanta began to say in a weary voice that he'd have to forgive her, that up till then she'd been lying, Señor Mallarino, and the entire visit was an act, for she was not a journalist, nor was she interested in interviewing him, nor was she an admirer of his, but she'd had to invent the whole lie, the false identity and pretend interest, to get inside this house and walk around it and look for that strange head she'd seen only once before, many years earlier, when she was a little girl and her life was made up of certainties, when she was a little girl and she had her whole life ahead of her.

TWO

There are women who do not preserve, on the map of their face, any trace of the little girl they once were, perhaps because they've made great efforts to leave childhood behind—its humiliations, its subtle persecutions, the experience of constant disappointment—perhaps because something's happened in the meantime, one of those private cataclysms that don't mold a person but rather raze them, like a building, and force them to reconstruct themselves from scratch. Mallarino looked at Samanta Leal and hunted in her features for some shape (the curve of the frontal bone where it reaches the space between the eyebrows, the way the earlobe joins the head) or perhaps an expression he'd seen on the face of the child twenty-eight years ago. And he could not: that child had gone, as if she'd refused to go on living in that face. Although it was true, on the other hand, that he'd seen her only once, and over the space of a very few hours, and perhaps his memory, which had always allowed him to recall the essential features of any face with a surgeon's precision, was now starting to deteriorate. If that were the case, the deterioration could not be less opportune, for now Samanta Leal, from whose face a little girl had vanished, was urgently asking him to remember that little girl and her visit to this house in the mountains in July of 1982, and not just that, but also the circumstances of that long-ago visit, the names and distinguishing marks of those present that afternoon, everything Mallarino saw and heard but also (if possible) what the rest of them saw and heard. "Remember, please," Samanta Leal said to him. "I need you to jog your memory." And he thought of that curious turn of phrase, *to jog a memory*, as if memory were something we could take out and exercise, or nudge into action, by way of certain well-chosen materials, by the mere effort of physical work. Memory would then be one of those horrible fountains sold by the roadside from the quarries in the hills, and that anyone could bring to life if they had talent and tools and obstinacy. Mallarino knew it wasn't like that, and yet here he was now, trying to extract the sculpture from the stone, sitting in front of a woman awaiting an answer beside the now darkened window. The whole house leaned over the glowing city, as if spying on it; Mallarino saw the luminous stitches against the black background—the city converted into a backlit, embroidered piece of fabric—and, in the distance, floating in the night air, planes waiting their turn to land, and he thought about the men and women who at that moment were occupying those illuminated spaces and trying, like him, to remember: remember something important, remember something banal, but always to remember; that's what we all devote ourselves to, all the time, that's where our meager energies go. *It's a poor sort of memory that only works backwards,* he thought again, and again he wondered where those words came from. That's what this was about, looking back and bringing the past toward us. "Please remember," Samanta Leal had said to him. Bit by bit, memory by memory, Mallarino was remembering.

Back then he had just moved to the house in the mountains. The move had been, more than a mere change of location, a sort of last resort, a desperate attempt to preserve, by way of the strategy of separation and distance, the well-being of his family. When had this moment begun brewing? With the anonymous threat, perhaps, with the violent imbalance that had followed it? For the first time Magdalena had asked him the question that he, silently, asked himself every day: Was it worth it? Were the fear and the risk and the antagonism and the threat worth it? "I'm not sure," said Magdalena. "I'm not sure it is worth it. You'll know, but think of our daughter. And think of me.

I don't know if it is worth it." Mallarino took her words as a betrayal—a tiny betrayal, but a betrayal in any event. Had the slow and imperceptible deterioration of their relationship, that two-humped monster called a couple that for more than a decade had behaved so well, started then? But it was impossible to say, thought Mallarino, impossible to spread the years of a marriage across a table like a map and draw a chalk circle around the precise moment, as the poet Silva had asked his doctor to draw a circle on the exact location of his heart. Of course Silva, after visiting the doctor, arrived home, took off his shirt, and shot himself in the exact center of the circle: that's why he'd sought the anatomy lesson—to commit an efficient suicide. Mallarino would have wanted something else: to repair, to eliminate from the chain of life the harmful moment, the first comment that was no longer impatient but hostile, the first reply bathed in sarcasm, the first glance empty of all admiration.

Yes, that was it: the admiration had fallen from Magdalena's eyes. He realized that his wife's admiration had always nourished him, and finding himself suddenly without it felt too much like a public slap in the face. The revelation struck him as at once fascinating and cruel: the experience of the need, the loss of the perfect independence Mallarino had cultivated all his life, unbalanced him more than he would have expected. "I won't get into bed with anybody," he used to say: it was one of his catchphrases, a behavioral guide, and Mallarino had turned to it several times to justify himself. When his cartoon was an attack on some friend of the family, or an associate of his father's (ruining a business, raising doubts about his father, presenting him to the world as a man incapable of earning the loyalty of his son), Mallarino received the more or less angry complaints with strained indifference, putting his art and his commitment—those are the words he used; he felt they protected him—above mere personal observances. "Merely personal?" Magdalena said once. *"Merely personal? But these people are our friends, Javier."* "Well, let's change friends," he replied. "And family? Should we change families too?" "If it comes to that," said Mallarino. "My credibility is at stake." *My reputation is at stake,* he thought without saying. And the sacrifices had worked: his reputation was there, his good reputation and his prestige. Mallarino had earned them the hard way; he didn't get into bed with anybody.

The sacrifices: Who had used that word for the first time, and in what circumstances? It was true that they no longer went to any of the posh restaurants in the north end, for they ran the risk of bumping into the victim of a cartoon or their more or less aggressive relatives, and it was true that a sort of permanent tension had settled over Sunday lunches with the family, a general and unnameable tension like the feeling that overwhelms us when there is someone dying in the next room; but it was no less true, and this is how Mallarino felt, that the people (that abstraction, a host of vague, featureless faces) respected and loved him. "And they need me," he said once. "They need someone to tell them what to think." "Don't be naive," Magdalena told him. "People already know what they think. People already have their prejudices well formed. They only want someone in authority to confirm their prejudices, even if it's the mendacious authority of newspapers. There's your prestige, Javier: you give people the wherewithal to confirm what they already think." She thought for a moment, or seemed to be thinking, then added: "You could have been a great artist. A Botero. An Obregón. You could have been one of the current ones, a Luis Caballero, a Darío Morales. You chose to be something else. You chose to be this: someone who gets us into trouble, who obliges us to fight with everybody, and who obliges everybody to fight with us." When had Magdalena changed so much? When had she stopped being the independent woman who had confronted a newspaper editor's censorship? "I don't want my daughter to grow up surrounded by people who have fallen out with her," Magdalena said. "I don't want her to annoy people who've never even seen her." Perhaps that's when Mallarino put the accusation into words: "Don't bring the child into this," he said to her. "The problem is much simpler. The problem is that you no longer admire me." Magdalena's only reply was a horsey snort that concentrated, in that instant, all the contempt in the world and all the invisible but obstinate deterioration in their relationship.

Mallarino would always remember the vehement urge to look for Beatriz to see if she had witnessed the scene, if she'd perceived the slight. It amazed him that his daughter, just turned seven, could share with them the spaces of the wreckage without realizing that her life was becoming a different one; it amazed him that her small, long-legged body could move through the rooms so confidently, that her eyes, under her arched brows, inherited from her mother, scrutinized the world, the infinite world, of her family silently but intensely, in that ferocious and hungry apprenticeship of young life, and all without full awareness that those days—of the shouts and whispers of nocturnal disputes, of tense breakfasts with amplified sounds of cutlery on plates—would mark her irremediably, perhaps sowing a hard seed of mistrust in her relationship with her parents, perhaps distorting from that moment on and forever her way of loving or of being loved. Mallarino, meanwhile, went through his days feeling dead tired, and it seemed as though his body, moving through the familiar terrain of his house, was leaving bits of dry skin, like a snake, like a leper. There was in the apartment an air of nervous tension or anxiety. When Beatriz began licking her hands because they were so dry (the sole result of which was the saliva's drying them out even more, and the girl's licking them more), Mallarino knew that it was time to move out, for his well-intentioned presence, that inertia of years as a family, was only making things worse. He should go. One night, in front of the television, he told Magdalena. She was sitting on her cushion, legs crossed like a Turkish boy, her gaze fixed on the screen. The soap opera *Son of Ruth* was on; Magdalena had been offered a part, but she wasn't an actress, didn't know what to do with her face, with her hands, and turned down the offer. "I work in radio," she'd told them, "only in radio." Now she regretted it.

"I'll move out for a while, a short while," Mallarino said.

Magdalena agreed.

"Just for a while. To see what happens."

"It's better this way. Better for everyone."

"We have to think of Beatriz."

"Yes. We have to think of Beatriz."

It didn't take long to find the house in the mountains. It was a unique opportunity, for the property was part of a disputed inheritance that would take some three years to be ruled on, meaning that Mallarino, with the help of the newspaper's lawyers, was able to sign an unusual, and unusually favorable, contract: he acquired possession of the house and began a series of necessary renovations, and until the inheritance was sorted out he would pay a fee the equivalent of a low rent; if the seller lost ownership of the house and the deal was no longer valid, Mallarino would get everything he paid back, including the cost of the renovations. The arrangement seemed made to measure for him: Mallarino was sure his separation from Magdalena would be short—when he tried to imagine how long it might last, on the basis of what had happened with other couples they knew, he thought in terms of months, maybe a year, two at most—and silently desired that the pending inheritance not work out, as if that legal situation had a secret link to the health of his marriage. At the end of June, between cartoons of a scandalously sacked Argentine soccer player (a big shock of dark hair and a karate suit) and of the British prime minister (the toothy smile, medieval armor, flag planted on a desert island), Mallarino bought a bed for thirty thousand pesos and a color TV from Sears, packed up a couple of thousand books in cardboard boxes, and covered his desk and instruments in bubble wrap. He also took personal charge of the collection of framed fetishes: the phrase *A stinger dipped in honey* that a carpenter had seared into a panel of wood, his Daumier reproductions—*The Legislative Belly* and *Past, Present, Future*—the oil painting of Magdalena with Beatriz in her arms like a Bellini Virgin, and the Rendón drawing, an old birthday present, in which the commissar asks the communist if he was planning to kill the president with those bombs and the communist replies: "Oh no, sir! We were hoping the president would be killed by remorse."

Everything was done carefully, the way people move a table with a vase on it: nobody wanted to commit a blunder, to be responsible for damage that could not be mended. They explained to Beatriz that from now on she'd have two houses, two bedrooms, two places to play, and she listened to them with patience but without looking at them, while popping plastic bubbles with her intensely concentrating thumb and forefinger. "She pretends it doesn't matter to her, but she is suffering," said Magdalena. And Mallarino: "But it's better this way." And Magdalena: "Yes. It's better this way." When the little girl's school holidays began, the move was complete; Beatriz lay down for the first time in her new bed, wrinkling her last day's uniform against the sheets, with trembling eyelids from too many farewell-party sweets, and Mallarino stayed there with his head on her pillow, breathing her breath, until he could tell she'd fallen asleep. He thought he'd get a group of friends together to celebrate the move—not because the move was worthy of celebration, but because a public, social event would normalize the situation in the child's eyes, take away all the embarrassing aspects, convert it into something acceptable she could talk to her friends about. He made a few calls, asked his guests to make some more, told Beatriz to invite one of her classmates. The following Sunday, at lunchtime, the new house was teeming with people, and Mallarino congratulated himself for having that splendid idea. Nothing would have allowed him to anticipate what happened next.

It was a sunny day; the sunshine was strong and dry and unusual for that time of year, and the doors of the house were wide open. Above their heads a ghost of a wind was blowing, audible in the leaves of the eucalyptus trees and the groaning of long branches. Mallarino walked through the rooms on the ground floor with a sense of detachment, as if he were the visitor, not the others. He had never been the host of a party. Magdalena had organized parties: she was the one who chose the food and moved one or two pieces of furniture to make it easier for people to circulate, and she was the one who welcomed the guests and took coats and left them, with considered carelessness, on their bed, and she took charge of making introductions, of the casual phrase that would start a conversation between two people who'd never set eyes on each other before, and people invariably lent themselves to those games, unaware of the power Magdalena's voice had over them and sometimes not even knowing that her voice was the same one that had held them spellbound to some radio station in some solitary moment of the week. (He had often thought that people's fondness for Magdalena was owing to that: they'd heard her in melancholy or lonely moments, and her voice had told them stories and had calmed them and allowed them not to think of their problems, of their latest failure, of the pretence of their success. Later they saw her and couldn't explain why her personality was so magnetic or her way of speaking so attractive.) But today Magdalena wasn't there. She had refused, subtly, affectionately, to come. She had thought it best, so Beatriz would start to get used to the division in her life, get used to inhabiting parallel universes in which one of her two parents didn't exist and had no reason to exist. Beatriz, for her part, seemed to accept the matter naturally: she had come to the door when her friend arrived, completely in possession of her role as woman of the house, and she herself asked her friend's mother if Samanta could sleep over. Samanta Leal, Beatriz's friend was called: a girl who was even shyer than she was, with deep green eyes, a small but fleshy mouth, and one of those little noses that has not yet begun to reveal what it will eventually become, all framed by the fringe of an old-fashioned doll. She was wearing a little gray schoolgirl's skirt (Mallarino thought that those knees would not be so clean or so unblemished by the end of the afternoon) and burgundy

patent leather shoes over ankle socks. She didn't look anything like her mother, who came inside briefly—she came
in the way mothers come into houses: to see that everything was or seemed to be fine, to check, as far as was
possible, that her daughter was not in any danger in this
unfamiliar environment—and looked at the bare walls
and paintings leaning against them, still wrapped in pro-
tective paper. "I just moved in," Mallarino told her (an ex-
planation not asked for). "Yes, I know," said the woman,
but didn't clarify how she knew. She was wearing brown
leather knee-high boots and an ochre coat, and on the
lapel of the coat a silver brooch in the shape of a dragonfly.
"So your wife's not here," said the woman, and then tried
to rephrase: "Beatriz's mother, I mean. She's not here?"

"She's coming later," said Mallarino. It wasn't true:
Magdalena would come to pick Beatriz up the next day.
But Mallarino felt that little white lie was convenient at
that moment, that it would reassure Samanta's mother or
save her some unnecessary worries.

"To collect Beatriz?"

"Yes, to pick her up. But not till later, the girls have
time to play."

"Oh, that's good. Well, Samanta's dad will come and
get her. He'll be coming, not me. What would be a good
time?"

"Whenever he likes," said Mallarino. "But tell him to come with time to spare. If Samanta is anything like my daughter, it's going to take a while to get her out of here."

The woman did not react to Mallarino's humor, and he thought: She's one of those. This was confirmed as they said good-bye, when, after shaking his hand and beginning to walk away, the woman turned halfway around and asked, almost over her shoulder: "You're the caricaturist, aren't you?"

"That's right, I'm the caricaturist," said Mallarino.

"Yes, that's who you are," said Samanta's mother. "I was trying to find out where I was bringing her." It seemed as though she was going to say something more, but what followed was an uncomfortable silence. A dog barked. Mallarino looked but couldn't spot it; he saw that another guest had arrived. "Well then, I'll leave her in your care," said the woman. "And thanks."

Now Mallarino had lost sight of them. He saw them pass by now and then, and once in a while he heard and recognized Beatriz's voice, her unmistakable, delicate little tone, and now and then he sensed, with some part of his awareness, the footsteps of both girls together, the nervous, quick, and distant steps, so distant from the adult world. Mallarino poured himself a whiskey, took a sip that tasted of wood, and felt a burning in the pit of his stomach. He went out into the tiny garden, where the guests seemed to be more numerous than they actually were, looked up, and closed his eyes briefly to feel the sun on his face, and like that, with his eyes closed, counted one, two clouds, or two shadows that flew across the curtain of sky. He liked this garden: Beatriz would be able to enjoy herself here. On the stairs he had to be careful not to kick over an ashtray full of cigarette butts; farther away, beside the wall, someone had dropped a piece of meat that was now sullying the place, like dog shit. Beside the rose bed was Gabriel Santoro, a professor at Rosario University, who had brought his son and a woman with a foreign accent, and farther away, near a pile of tiles left over from the renovations that hadn't been taken away yet, Ignacio Escobar was talking to a newsreader and her most recent boyfriend. Monsalve, maybe, or maybe Manosalbas: Mallarino had forgotten his name. Was it possible there were fewer acquaintances than strangers at this get-together? And if that was true, what did it mean? "Oh, finally," Rodrigo Valencia said as he saw him approach. "Come here, Javier, come and drink a toast with us, damn it, or do you not speak to your guests, sir." Rodrigo Valencia never addressed anyone informally, not even his own children, but his way of speaking was so physical—made up of interjections and slaps on the back, heavy hands on shoulders, exaggerated bows—that nobody felt deprived of his closeness or trust. He hugged Javier and said: "This fellow is going to be the greatest, mark my words. He's already great, but he's going to be the greatest. Mark my words." The recipients of this prophesy, each with a glass of *aguardiente* in hand, were Elena Ronderos, Valencia's wife, and a columnist for *El Independiente*, Gerardo Gómez, who had just returned from an eighteen-month exile in Mexico. Like Mallarino, he'd received an anonymous threat; but in his case, for reasons no one really understood, the police had considered it prudent for him to go away somewhere while things calmed down. "Until stuff calms down, that's what they told me," said Gómez. "Not you? Have they never told you to go away?"

"Never," said Mallarino. "Who knows why."

"Maybe because drawings aren't as direct," said Gómez.

"But more people see them," said Valencia.

"But they're not as direct," said Gómez. "And subtlety is not these people's strong suit. Hey, Javier, what happens if they send another one?"

"They're not going to send any more," said Mallarino. "It's been almost a year."

"But what if they do send something else? You have to think about what you'd do."

"They're not going to send anything," said Mallarino.

"How can you be so sure?" said Gómez. "You're not going soft on us, are you?"

"Your father'll go soft before this one," said Valencia, who was allowed to say such things. "Didn't you see last Sunday's cartoon? A depth charge, Gómez, a depth charge, and I'm not saying that because Mallarino is here. The drawing was a marvel, worthy of Goya. A bizarre thing, a sort of bat with the face of the treasury minister. And underneath, it said: 'We had to frighten people to reassure the markets.' What do you think? We've already received several calls from the ministry, from the minister's press office. They're furious! So don't give us that, Gómez, nobody's getting soft. Don't go thinking . . ."

Gerardo Gómez interrupted him: "What's that guy doing here?"

He was looking toward the front door, past the sliding door to the garden that reflected the trees and the clear sky and people's clothing, past the big armchair where Beatriz and her friend were playing some private game, beyond the back of the leather sofa and the coffee table with its art books and empty vase and small army of abandoned glasses of *aguardiente*. A man had just come in; he had stopped in the middle of the living room, looking off into space, as if he were waiting for someone, but Mallarino knew he wasn't looking off into space but at the fireplace, or rather the wall above the fireplace, the wide white space inhabited by the single painting Mallarino had had time to hang: one of his first nudes of Magdalena, painted at the beginning of the seventies or even earlier, before they were married, when Magdalena's body was still a discovery. Nobody could tell it was her, because the woman in the painting had her face hidden in the pillows, but the man was looking at her (looking at the messy sheets with their different tones of white, the naked torso, and the beauty spot on the left breast, beside the relaxed nipple) as if he'd recognized her by way of some mysterious art. Mallarino, for his part, recognized him: it was Adolfo Cuéllar, a Conservative congressman he'd drawn many times over the last few years and with a certain frequency a few months back, enough to know now by heart his large ears, the childish freckles on his face, and the severe line of his slicked-over hair. His reputation had turned him into a target of several attacks from the liberal press. Few public men carried their reputations the way Cuéllar carried his, standing on his shoulder like a parrot—no, draped around his neck the way a snake charmer carries his snake. Maybe that's what a reputation is: the moment when a presence fabricates, for those observing, an illusory precedent. Mallarino's last caricature had appeared after a nurse had been beaten to death by her husband with a large hoe in a village in Valledupar. "It's very regrettable," Cuéllar said into a journalist's microphone. "But when someone hits a woman, it's generally for a reason." Mallarino had drawn him standing in a forest of tombstones, with an oversize head on which his freckles and hair were easily distinguished, wearing a three-piece suit, and carrying a garden hoe in one hand; in the background, sitting on a rock in a posture denoting insurmountable tedium, was Death with his long black cloak and his scythe held in his folded arms. *When one is out of work,* read the line beneath the image, *it's generally for a reason.* And now the man—"the man of the hoe," as a columnist had already called him in the magazine *Semana*—was in Mallarino's house. "What's that guy doing here?" Gerardo Gómez had asked. "That's what I'd like to know," said Mallarino. Or maybe he didn't get the whole sentence out: "That's what I'd like . . ." he managed to say, and at that moment he saw Rodrigo Valencia wipe his mouth with a paper napkin (above his upper lip, a trail of white specks had stuck to his badly shaven skin) and clear his throat, with a touch of comic intent. "I invited him," said Valencia. "*Mea culpa,* Javier, I forgot to warn you."

"What do you mean you invited him?" said Mallarino.

"He called me on Friday, man, he called to beg me. That he needed to speak to Señor Mallarino. That I had to get him a meeting with Señor Mallarino. He pestered me so damn much he left me no choice."

"Wait one second. A *meeting?*"

"You've got to understand, man. It was like the guy was on his knees over the phone."

"But on a Sunday?" said Mallarino. "Today? Sunday? Here in my house? Have you gone mad, Rodrigo?"

"There was no other way to get rid of him. He's a congressman, Javier."

"He's an idiot."

"He's a congressional idiot," said Valencia. "Speak to him for two seconds, that's all I'm asking. At least the guy was civil enough to show up after lunch."

"Not to eat my food, you mean."

"Exactly, Javier," said Valencia. "Not to eat your food."

Mallarino went inside out of courtesy (the host advancing to receive the recent arrival) and at the same time as prevention (to keep the recent arrival from being seen in the place where the party was taking place and feeling, mistakenly, that he was welcome there). He greeted Cuéllar: a chubby, flaccid hand, a gaze that fixed on Mallarino's left shoulder. His hair was shorter than it seemed from a distance: Mallarino saw the broad forehead, completely clear, a slight smudge of Brylcreem on the left temple, a fruit fly caught in a spiderweb, and later, seeing him turn around to sit down, he noticed a bulge at the back of his head, as if something were struggling to get out of there (something ugly, no doubt: a secret, a devious past). Everything about the little man made him feel an intense disgust: he was grateful to be taller than him, thinner, more elegant in spite of his inattention to his wardrobe. "Thanks for seeing me, Javier," the little man was saying. "On a Sunday, for crying out loud, and you with guests."

"My pleasure," said Mallarino. "But I would ask you not to call me by my first name. You and I don't know each other."

There was a sort of clumsiness in the man's movements. "No, of course," he said. "Precisely." And then: "Can I take my jacket off?"

He did, and Mallarino found himself looking at a linen waistcoat with a blue-and-green diamond pattern straining violently over a prominent potbelly. Mallarino, in his caricatures, had never taken advantage of these recently discovered curves, and thought he would the next time. He led Cuéllar to a corner of the room, closest to the kitchen, and there, on two chairs not positioned to be used, but just to go with the telephone table, they sat down to talk. Mallarino felt around and turned on the lamp: in this part of the house, far from the big window overlooking the garden, you could tell that evening was starting to fall. The yellow light illuminated Cuéllar's face and bones and skin, which cast new shadows as he moved. Cuéllar bent over to adjust one of his loafers (maybe it was swallowing his sock, thought Mallarino, that could be very uncomfort-

able) and then straightened up again. "Look, Señor Mallarino," he began to say, "I wanted to meet you, wanted us to
meet, because it seems to me that you have a, how should I
put this, a mistaken image. Of me, of course. A mistaken
image of me." Mallarino listened to him while looking for
a couple of clean glasses and poured two double shots of
whiskey, a matter of not neglecting his duties as host even
for a man unworthy of them. From the garden came the
sound of a woman's loud laugh: Mallarino looked up to see
who it was; Cuéllar, however, wiped his palms on his trousers, his fingers spread out as if he hoped Mallarino would
notice the cleanliness of his nails, and kept talking. "I am
not the person you draw in your caricatures. I'm different.
You don't know me." "That's what I just said," said Mallarino, "you and I don't know each other." "We don't know
each other," said Cuéllar. "And it seems to me that you've
been unfair to me, forgive my saying. I'm not a bad person,
you understand? I'm a good person. Ask my wife. Ask my
children. I have two, two boys. Ask them and you'll see
they'll say so, that I'm a good person. Poor little guys. I
don't show them your drawings. My wife doesn't show
them, forgive me for telling you this, sorry."

Mallarino could barely believe it: the man had come
on a supplicant mission. *He called to beg me,* Valencia had
said, *it was like the guy was on his knees over the phone.*
Mallarino felt invaded by a solid contempt, as palpable as a

tumor. What was annoying him so much? Was it perhaps the humility with which Adolfo Cuéllar was speaking to him, head bent, casting a shadow under his nose, arms resting on his knees (the pose of someone confessing to a friendly priest, a sinner before his confessor), or perhaps the respect with which Cuéllar was treating him in spite of the fact that Mallarino obviously felt none? I've humiliated him, I've ridiculed him, and now he's come to lick my ass. What a repugnant man. Yes, that was it, an unpredictable and thus more intense repugnance, a repugnance for which Mallarino was not prepared. He had expected complaints, protests, even diatribes; a few minutes earlier he had greeted this man with a measure of hostility just to better face up to the other's hostility, like an employee who, caught in the wrong, arrives at the supervisor's office gesticulating and shouting, launching little precautionary attacks. Well, now it seemed that Cuéllar had come here not to demand the immediate cessation of those aggressive drawings but to humiliate himself even further before his aggressor. He is an adult, thought Mallarino, a grown man, and I have humiliated him; he has a wife and kids and I have ridiculed him, and this adult man does not defend himself, this head of a family does not respond with similar blows but humiliates himself even more, seeks even more ridicule. Mallarino found himself feeling a confusing emotion that went beyond contempt, something that wasn't irritation or annoyance but seemed dangerously close to hatred, and it alarmed him to be feeling it. "Please, Javier, please don't draw me like that anymore. I'm not like that," Cuéllar was saying. "That's what I came to ask you, Señor Mallarino," he corrected himself with a shaky and nervous voice (nervous like Beatriz when she licked the dry skin of her hands), "thank you for listening to me, sorry for your time, I mean thank you for your time." Mallarino listened to him and thought: He's weak. He's weak and that's why I hate him. He's weak and I'm strong now, and I hate him for making the fact so obvious, for allowing me to abuse my strength, for giving me away, yes, for exposing this power that maybe I don't deserve. Seen from this seat, the sliding door to the garden had turned into a big illuminated rectangle, and Mallarino saw, against the bright backdrop, the silhouettes that now began to enter. "The day's cooled down now," he heard someone say. The house filled with lively conversations, open and more discreet laughter; someone asked where the record player was, and someone else, Gómez or Valencia, began to sing without waiting for musical accompaniment. *I saw you arrive,* he sang, *and felt the presence of an unknown being:* it was a song Magdalena liked, but there was no way Valencia or Gómez knew that or knew that those lines were forcing Mallarino to remember his absent wife, the profound emptiness that was opening in his life without her, and to regret everything, to regret it intensely: *I saw you arrive and felt what I'd never, ever felt before.* Adolfo Cuéllar was just apologizing again: for taking Mallarino's time, for invading his house on a Sunday. He was talking about a father's image for his children, and how his sons would grow up with Mallarino's image of him. "Do it for them," Cuéllar was saying, "as a father yourself, please," he asked, or begged, and Mallarino saw his ears, his nose, the bones of his forehead and temples, and thought of the strange disdain those bones and cartilage produced in him, and said to himself that even if Adolfo Cuéllar didn't strike him as a repugnant little character, he would keep drawing him nonstop, and his bones and cartilage were to blame. His bones are to blame, thought Mallarino, it's always all the fault of bones and cartilage. And then: Bones are the only things that matter; in them, in the shape of the skull and the angle of the nose, in the width of the forehead and the strength or trepidation of a jaw and the dimples on a chin, their delicate or brusque slopes, their more or less intense shadows, there lies the reputation and the image: give me a bone and I shall move the world. Politicians don't know it, they haven't realized yet, or maybe they have, but it's not something they can fix: we are born with these bones, it's very difficult to change them, and so we'll go through life with the same vulnerabilities, or always forcing ourselves to compensate for them. Didn't someone say that a successful man is simply someone who has found the way to conceal a complex? In the living room, standing next to a crouching body that was manipulating old newspapers to light, for the first time, a fire in the fireplace of the new house, Rodrigo Valencia—it was him, it was Valencia, now Mallarino had recognized him—was singing at the top of his voice the lines of the song about a love that wasn't fire and wasn't flame, and those other lines, which Magdalena loved so much, about the distances that separate cities and cities that destroy customs, and with each line Mallarino had the impression that Adolfo Cuéllar, who now took a sip of his drink and made a grotesque grimace as he swallowed, fell lower and lower in humiliation and shamelessness. A burst of flames reddened the room. Cuéllar was incredible: How could he inflict such pains on himself, or was he not overwhelmed by any pain at kneeling before someone who'd wounded him? Mallarino was on the verge of asking him roughly when there was a sound of breaking glass, and before Mallarino had time to discover where it had come from, Elena Ronderos appeared, taking long strides and moving her hands as if wiping a clumsy phrase off a blackboard.

"Hey, Javier, come quick," she said. "Something's wrong with the girls."

And that's how the adults discovered that Beatriz and her little friend had spent the last hour running around the house, visiting every surface where there were half-finished drinks, every table in the living room and every step on the stairs and every shelf where some guest might have set down the last sip of *aguardiente* or whiskey or rum, and now they were so drunk they were splayed out like pinned butterflies on the floor of Beatriz's room and couldn't even open their eyes or answer any of the questions they were asked. They had broken one of the framed pictures that were propped up against the wall, waiting to be assigned a place, and there was the frame and three or four long triangles of glass. Mallarino thought he'd clean them up right away, but first he picked up his daughter; someone, he didn't know who, picked up Samanta Leal, and a few seconds later both girls were on the bed in the master bedroom, one beside the other like two pens on a sheet of drawing paper, perfectly unconscious and motionless. A woman whose name Mallarino didn't remember brought a wet cloth from the kitchen; she put it on the girls' foreheads, alternately, and on Beatriz's and Samanta's pale skin, on their foreheads, emptied of color, was a fleeting patch, red and damp. Mallarino, meanwhile, had called a pediatrician, and moments later, he was striding into the room and sitting on the edge of the bed and setting down on the bedside table, or rather on top of his notebook, transforming it into a coaster, a glass of water with sugar and a teaspoon that glistened when he turned on the reading lamp. "A little bit every twenty minutes and everything will be fine," he said. "A little spoonful, just one, and everything will be fine."

We got drunk?" said Samanta Leal. "I got drunk?"

"You two drank all the dregs in the house," said Mallarino. "And it wasn't funny either. You could have put yourselves in a coma."

"I don't remember at all. I don't remember your daughter. Were we very good friends?"

"Not as far as I know. Beatriz changed best friends every week. That's what it's like when you're seven, I guess."

"I guess," said Samanta. "And who looked after us, you?"

"Every twenty minutes I looked in on you," said Mallarino, "and gave you each a teaspoonful of sugar water. That's what the doctor had told me to do. You wouldn't believe how hard it was to get you to swallow it."

"I don't remember, I don't remember at all."

"Of course not. You were both out of it, Samanta, completely out. At one point I even put a mirror under your nostrils, to make sure you hadn't died on me. A father's paranoia."

"Nobody dies of that."

"No, of course not, but what did I know? Or rather, a father imagines anything, that anything might be possible. And you looked like you'd fainted."

"Well, we must have."

"We couldn't hear you breathing. You didn't even snore the way drunks do. You didn't move either. It was as if you were sedated. I put a blanket over you both, one of those blankets people used to steal from airplanes, and the blanket didn't even move: each time I came back it was exactly as I'd left it, I think I could have painted the scene and the folds would have stayed exactly the same for as long as it took. As I said, you were both out cold. Naturally."

"Naturally?"

"I mean, that much booze in a seven-year-old body, and not just any drinks but *aguardiente* and rum. You might as well have just been gulping down a coma. No, but we really were very worried. And you don't remember a thing."

"Nothing at all."

"I see that."

"Not a thing," said Samanta.

"Not about what happened afterward either?" Silence. "The scandal, all that? You don't remember that either?" Silence. "I see," said Mallarino. "So that's what this . . ."

"Yes," said Samanta. "It's about that."

"I see." Silence. "But you must remember something."

Samanta closed her eyes. "I remember my dad lifting

me up," she said. "Or maybe not, maybe I only think I remember my dad lifting me up, because I remember my dad putting me in the car, in the backseat of the car. And if he carried me to the car, he must have had to lift me up, right? My dad carried me to the car, didn't he?"

"I think so."

"You don't know?"

"I don't remember too clearly," said Mallarino. "I was very upset, you know. Everybody was very upset at that moment."

"Because of the drinks," said Samanta. It wasn't a question; it wasn't even an affirmation. It was something else.

"No, no," said Mallarino. "You know that's not why. The upset over the drinks had passed by then, you two were sleeping and taken care of, I was going in every twenty minutes with my spoonful of sugar water. That was under control."

"So then?"

"You know," said Mallarino.

"No," said Samanta, "that's just it. I don't know." Silence. "And what I want is to know. I want you to tell me." Silence. "Let's see, let's see. You were taking care of us."

"Yes."

"You came by with spoonfuls of sugar water."

"Yes."

"Every twenty minutes."

"Yes. That's what the doctor ordered."

"And between one spoonful and the next?"

"I went to see to my guests, of course. I was still the host."

"They were all still there?"

"Most of them, at least. I don't remember anyone having left."

"Were they all there when my father arrived?"

"I think so. As I said, most of them. I had just given you two a spoonful, but I don't remember if it was the third or fourth. There was a fire lit in the fireplace, I remember that, and I had to keep it burning. I went out to the garden, brought in wood, looked for old newspapers to burn, and the fire kept burning. People had taken over the bar—I mean they knew where to find booze and were helping themselves. But now and then someone asked me for something: ice, a fresh glass, soda, cigarettes. I remember that: the smell of cigarette smoke. Or I think I remember that, but maybe it's just because I had stopped smoking. Anyway, what I can tell you is that I didn't sit down for a second. Between the fireplace, the things people asked me for, and friends who put their arm over my shoulders to sing a *ranchera*, I didn't sit down for a second. I don't even remember having answered the door when your father arrived. Introducing him, yes: I remember introducing him, making him come into the living room where everybody was and introducing him, *Look, Samanta's dad, yes, Samanta, Beatriz's little friend.* And everybody stiffening, obviously: he had to be told something, but nobody wanted to be the one to tell him. That's when I realized I'd screwed up. I should have explained the whole thing as soon as I opened the door. But I don't know if I answered the door, Samanta, maybe the door was open and he just walked in. That changes everything, don't you think? When you answer the door to a stranger, it's easier for something to occur to you, to explain something important to someone you don't know. But if the stranger finds himself suddenly inside, you might forget, no? Some tiny distraction, any little thing . . . It doesn't matter, it's not an excuse. I should have explained everything as soon as I shook his hand. But I didn't, and it was a mistake."

"Why was it a mistake?"

"Because it put him on the defensive. Don't take this the wrong way, Samanta, but as soon as I saw him I realized that your dad wasn't the most assured guy in the world. Or isn't. He's still alive, I imagine."

"I was fifteen when he left. I know at first he was living in Brazil, then I haven't heard anything since. What do you mean by 'assured'?"

"I mean you could see a sort of bashfulness from a mile away, I don't know how to explain it, something that made him pull back. You could see that he would rather not have come to pick you up, that he would have preferred it if your mother had come. I introduced him to everybody in the living room and it seemed hard for him to shake hands, and it was very strange, a guy that size so reticent. He's a big guy, your dad, a well-built guy, and there in the living room, with all of us, he seemed sort of shrunken. Your dad seemed like one of those big guys who would rather not draw attention to themselves when they arrive, and seem to have their head ducked down between their shoulders, as if they were bending down to go through a low door. Although maybe it's always like that, you know? Maybe that's always the way it is with someone who just arrives at a party where everybody's had a bit to drink. You look small even if you're six feet tall and have swimmer's shoulders—at least that's how I remember your dad. I also remember long sideburns and a strong jawline. I may be mistaken. You have a strong jawline, Samanta, but not like your dad's. In any case, after I finished making the rounds, introducing him to all those people who stared at him, I explained what had happened. The look on his face changed, of course. Where was Samanta, he began asking me, where was his daughter? 'She's upstairs, in my room,' I told him. 'She's fine, don't worry, she's asleep and she's fine, both of them are fine, my daughter too.' That was to remind him that there were two little girls with the same problem, not just one, and if I was here, relatively calm, he could be here too, relatively calm. 'And where are the stairs?' he asked me. I pointed toward the hallway, just as I pointed it out to you a few hours ago, and said, 'Give me a second, I'll come with you.' But he didn't give me a second. I don't remember him running, or even walking quickly, as one does in an emergency. No, no: he simply turned on his heel, without saying anything to me, a little offended, I think, or indignant, and went toward the staircase without another word. He didn't have to say anything for me to know what he was thinking. *What kind of place is this,* that's what he was thinking, *how did my daughter end up here?* There are people who don't know how to deal with the unexpected, and your dad was like that, you could see that too from a mile away. He walked toward the stairs and I saw him go through the doorway, there, on the left, just as we did before. And then I didn't see him anymore. I didn't follow him, Samanta, and now I'm very sorry that I didn't. But it bothered me, what can I say: his impoliteness, his rough edges bothered me. I thought: Okay then, to hell with him, he's on his own. Let him go upstairs, look around, try the wrong door, let him find her, see that everything's fine, throw her over his shoulder, and get out of here. To hell with him. That's what I thought. And then the shouting started."

"Coming from upstairs."

"It began upstairs," said Mallarino, "and then came

down the staircase, rolling down the stairs like a ball—no, like a stone, like one of those landslides you get on mountain roads. One time, when Beatriz was a baby, I ran into a landslide near La Nariz del Diablo. Have you seen the Devil's Nose, Samanta? It's on the way to the tropical lowlands, a huge piece of rock, truly gigantic, that juts out of the mountain and hangs over the road like a bridge. People say that the devil stands there, on top of that stone nose, to make cars crash. The drivers get scared or distracted and lose control and drive over the edge of the cliff, which is extremely high at that point, a cut through the mountain and a fall into the abyss. Down there at the bottom of the ravine are the cars of the victims, and if they don't die when they hit the bottom, they die for lack of help, because no one can get down that far, and if they shout, no one can hear them. . . . My wife and I were going to spend Easter week in Melgar, I think it was. Beatriz's first holiday. She was in the back, or rather they were both in the back, Magdalena with Beatriz in her arms. And we ran into the landslide. They'd closed the road a little ways before the Nariz and the traffic was stopped and we saw the Nariz, and Magdalena started talking about the devil. 'What if we see him?' she said. 'What if we see the devil standing right there?' We didn't see him, Samanta, we didn't see the devil, but we heard a noise and then everything started to tremble, the car began to tremble, and the landslide came down the mountain. A stampede of big rocks that seemed to be heading straight for us, to have us in their sights, and for four or five seconds one thinks, Well, that's it, here and no further, because if one of those rocks landed on top of us no car's bodywork would hold up. It all passed twenty meters ahead of us, but just thinking that Magdalena and Beatriz were back there . . . Anyway, a landslide is a shocking spectacle that would frighten anybody. So, like that landslide, the shouts came crashing down from upstairs. It still strikes me as incredible that neither of you woke up."

"I didn't wake up, at least I don't remember being woken up. And your daughter?"

"No. She was still out cold, in another world."

"Has she told you?"

"What?"

"Has she told you that she didn't hear anything?"

"Well, no," said Mallarino. "I've never asked her. We've never talked about that night. The truth is I've never talked about that night with anybody: I've never had any reason to. This is the first time in twenty-eight years, I mean, and the effort is not inconsiderable. I hope you'll keep that in mind."

"Tell me about the shouting."

"The shouts came pouring down the stairs like a landslide, Samanta. I don't know what went through my head, but I wasn't the only one: everyone in the room stopped what they were doing. Drinks were left on the table. Conversations ended mid-sentence. Those who were sitting stood up. In my memory even the music was turned off, but it's impossible that the music would have stopped automatically at that exact moment, and nevertheless I remember it like that: the music stopped playing. Your memory does things, you know? Your memory turns off music and gives people beauty spots and changes the locations of friends' houses. We began to walk toward the stairs, and at that moment Adolfo Cuéllar came down them. That's how I remember it: Cuéllar came down first. I don't know when he'd gone up, or what for. He hadn't asked me if he could see the upper floor of the house, or asked me where the bathroom was, or anything like that. One second he was there, in the living room with us, I don't know whether saying good-bye or looking for his coat that he'd taken off, if he'd been wearing a coat, and the next moment he was being chased down the stairs by Señor Leal's shouts. 'Hey,' he was shouting, 'hey, come here.' The shouts came in time with his footsteps, pummeling down the stairs like a landslide, Samanta, his loud and hurried footsteps. 'What happened here? What did you do to my little girl?' And what happened next I remember like this: all the guests in the corridor leading to the stairs, or a good many of us in the corridor and the rest out here, under that arch, there where the corridor begins. It was like a bottleneck, like a funnel. Cuéllar came down first. He passed me but I didn't stop him to ask him what was going on. It didn't seem necessary. Or maybe it didn't even occur to me. Your dad had come down by then too, and he was shouting at Cuéllar across the group of people: Valencia, Gómez, Santoro, Elena, a group that had gotten in between your dad and Cuéllar purely by instinct, the instinct to avoid a fight. And this is something I'm never going to forget: your dad wanted to smell Cuéllar's hands. That's what he was shouting: 'Give me your hands! Let me smell your hands!' And he kept insulting him: 'Let me smell your fingers, you son of a bitch!' I kept going toward the staircase and headed up. I needed to know what had happened. Or maybe that wasn't it: not that I needed to know what had happened but needed to make sure nothing had happened to Beatriz. At that moment Beatriz was much more important to me than you, what can I say. The door to my room was ajar, and I remember thinking, as I walked toward it, that it was odd, because if your dad had been here and had rushed out, wasn't it strange that he would have stopped to adjust the door? That's what I was thinking as I opened it. First I saw the blanket, the airline blanket, on the floor, and then I saw you, Samanta. I saw you still asleep, I mean unconscious, but lying faceup, not on your side as I'd left you last time, but lying faceup and with your skirt raised a little. You had your legs apart, or one leg bent, I think that was it, one leg bent. I looked away, out of discretion, you understand, but I didn't turn my head fast enough, and I did see something. Then I went around the bed to make sure Beatriz was all right. There I was, on the other side of the bed, crouched down by my daughter's face, when your father came in and with a quick glance held me responsible for everything. He lifted you up and carried you out. It looked perfectly normal, you with your arms around your daddy's neck, like all little girls and all fathers. But what wasn't normal was his left hand, which was gripping your bottom, not to support you, but as if covering you, covering up your underwear. I followed him down the stairs. The dogs had come in—I imagine they were attracted by the uproar—and had started to bark. You and your father left, and from the front door I watched you get in the car, or I watched him put you into the backseat, then get in himself and start the engine and put it in reverse. I remember it had started to rain, or to drizzle: I noticed when he turned on his headlights I suddenly saw drops. And I stood there for a moment, watching the raindrops floating in the air, and when the car had gone out through the gate I closed the door and went back inside and realized that Adolfo Cuéllar had left too. The dogs were still barking. The fire had gone out. Someone, I don't remember who, asked for his coat. People began to leave."

"And the party was over," said Samanta.

"Exactly," said Mallarino. "The next day I drew the caricature. And the day after that it was published."

In those days, subscribing to a newspaper was to expect, every morning, the transformation of the world, sometimes as a brutal jolt to all you knew, sometimes via subtle access to a removed reality: the shoemaker's shop visited by elves during the night. After his move, the first thing Mallarino had done was to make sure all the paperboys had the correct address, for one could do without coffee and without breakfast, without running water and without a phone, but not without the newspaper waiting on the doorstep, damp from the recent fog, still cold with the early-morning mountain chill, but ready for Mallarino to open, the way a child—still in his pajamas, sleep in the corners of his eyes—opens Christmas presents. Wasn't it Rockefeller who had them make him his own version of *The New York Times*, an adulterated version with all the bad news expunged? Mallarino had never been able to understand that: for him it was the indignation or rage or hatred that kept him alive. How could someone renounce the intense feeling of superiority one feels when hating

someone? It was the emotion that made mornings make
sense. That morning, Mallarino went directly to the opinion page. And there was his black-framed square, which
this time he'd drawn a little thicker, and in the center of
the box, a sort of promontory that looked like it was made
of earth, something like a small hill. At the base of the hill,
surrounding it, there was a crowd of heads with long
straight hair, all seen from the back, some adorned with a
girlish ribbon. On top of the hill, on the apex of the head-
land, was Adolfo Cuéllar—there were Adolfo Cuéllar's
bones and cartilages—dressed in a diamond-patterned
waistcoat, the lines of which were strained by the prominent belly. He had his arms open, as if wanting to embrace
the world, and his freckled face looked toward the sky.
Mallarino had written the caption the way Ricardo Rendón
used to: putting down for the record the name of the character, then a dash, then his fictitious words, as if the caption were the title of a novel, so that what was read—what
millions of people were reading at that very moment—on
the most-read page of *El Independiente*, was this:

CONGRESSMAN ADOLFO CUÉLLAR—
SUFFER THE LITTLE GIRLS TO COME UNTO ME.

It wasn't the first time Mallarino had drawn an "out-
of-context cartoon," as he called a caricature without an

obvious or immediate reference, such as a piece of news or something that was common knowledge. But it had never felt as natural as it did this time. The image had formed in his head the morning after the party, as soon as he had a moment of solitude in the new house and the strangeness forced him to take refuge in his work routine in order not to give in to melancholy. Still under the impression of the confrontation—it had been a confrontation, a moment of violence—he had woken up feeling like the victim of a brutal fatigue, like someone who'd just had an accident. The tension in his shoulders and neck, the tension in his waist, the pain of his hernia that appeared at moments like this and shot down his left leg . . . he took a long shower and then, still in his bathrobe, began to draw. He didn't feel indignation or rage but rather something more abstract, like disquiet, almost like the awareness of a possibility . . . of a power—yes, that was it: the awareness of an imprecise power. In twenty-five minutes, not counting the time it took to assemble his materials, the drawing was finished. Mallarino poured himself a beer, lit a cigarette, and sat in the garden with the novel he was reading at the time. "Last night," he read, "as I reached into the chest where I store my papers, the creatures climbed up my forearm, waving their little legs, their antennae, trying to get out into the fresh air." The reptiles crawled over the narrator's skin, and Mallarino thought of Cuéllar, remembered his pleading and his bones and his cartilage and his flattery, and the narrator meanwhile declared his infinite repugnance. And now that the caricature was out there in the real universe, where opinions have their effects and reputations are feeble, there was no turning back, nor did Mallarino want there to be.

Rodrigo Valencia was in the habit of phoning him on days a special caricature came out, because, even though he had seen and commented on the drawing the previous day, he thought it was not excessive to offer the cartoonist moral support when his work went out into the world. But this morning it wasn't Valencia who phoned first but Gerardo Gómez. "Oh man, that takes spunk," said Gómez. "And there I was asking if you'd gone soft on us. As if!" Valencia, who phoned next, thought it was a harsh but necessary declaration (or maybe he said denunciation): there were certain things that had to be said and only a caricature could say them correctly. "If you don't say it, nobody says it," he added. "Okay, go get some rest. Here at the office we're ready for whatever's coming." They didn't have long to wait for the calls of complaint: from Cuéllar's secretary, from a woman with a screechy voice, from a lawyer who claimed to be representing Cuéllar and determined to instigate the appropriate legal actions. "But don't worry, Javier, nothing's going to happen," said Valencia. "Suing over a cartoon is like admitting the charges. Besides, you're you, let's not kid ourselves, and this newspaper is this newspaper." There was a letter to the editor: "We protest in the most emphatic way . . . this unjust attack on the image of one of our most distinguished public servants. . . . We, who have ardently defended our fatherland, denounce the partisan use of the national means of communication. . . ." It was signed "Friends of Congressman Adolfo Cuéllar." For Mallarino, the fact that the letter was, in practice, anonymous, just as bombastic and falsely elegant as the anonymous threats, differing only in its lack of capital letters and its spelling mistakes, confirmed, in an imprecise, inexplicable, and maybe superstitious way, the validity of the drawing and what the drawing suggested. *What the drawing suggested:* neither declared nor denounced, thought Mallarino; it was like a whisper at a meeting, a sidelong glance. Caricatures had rare chemical properties: Mallarino gradually noticed that any defense that Cuéllar himself might make or that anyone else might make for him sank him further into disrepute, as if the true disgrace was mentioning the caricature. What was the mysterious mechanism that turned a journalistic attack into a kind of quicksand where simply making a fuss was enough to make one sink further and irremediably? Mallarino realized that by not tying his attack to a concrete and verifiable piece of news, by allowing himself to be rather gratuitous, he made defense impossible or ridiculous: it's impossible to answer something unsaid, unless you do so precisely by saying that thing. As if that were not enough, the gratuitous attack enjoyed a longer life. By the following Friday, when Magdalena brought Beatriz over to spend the weekend with her father, the caricature should have fallen into oblivion, dragged away or obliterated by current events, which never let up (the new president and his imminent inauguration, maybe, or the earthquake that had killed so many people in a small nearby country), or at least have passed down the list of that capricious and voluble monster, the newspaper reader's priorities. But that was not the case. It had not fallen into oblivion; it had not slipped down the list of priorities: it had taken on a life of its own and was wandering the city, loose and hazardous, ricocheting around corners.

Or that, at least, is what Magdalena wanted to say from the very moment of her arrival. Mallarino opened the door, said hello with a hug, felt a surge of desire as he touched her blue blouse: he'd always liked that blouse, the way it accentuated the curve of her breasts, and he briefly fantasized about the possibility that she had chosen it on purpose. A new sincerity had established itself between them since the incident: maybe, thought Mallarino, it was the awareness of the proximity of danger, of the bad things that had grazed their lives without touching them, for

Magdalena, with feminine wisdom, had overlooked Mallarino's inattention to the abandoned drinks to concentrate
on what happened afterward, which really was serious and
dangerous. She had something to tell him, Magdalena said
with a vague tension in the way she moved, would he mind
if she came in for a while? And there, both sitting at the
dining room table after eating with Beatriz (as they used
to do, thought Mallarino without saying so, as they used to
do in the world they had mislaid and would have to re-
cover), each holding a cup of steaming tea, as they waited
while the little girl showered and put her dirty clothes in
the hamper and cleaned her teeth with a toothbrush with
a handle the shape of a very skinny fairy, Magdalena de-
scribed a scene in which the opinion page of *El Independiente* appeared one day on the bulletin board at the Cuéllar
boys' school, and one of them, the eldest, got into a fistfight
with a classmate who made a disagreeable comment about
his father. "Can you imagine?" said Magdalena with something that might have been consternation but could also
mean something else. "At the school!" Mallarino was listening to her story, but his attention was not on it but
rather on the sudden complicity bathing them at that moment, a connection between them they hadn't felt for a
long time—or was it perhaps the rare emotion the joint
protection of a child produces? "Has she asked anything?"
said Mallarino. "Nothing," said Magdalena, "she hasn't

said anything." "And what about the Leal girl? Do we know anything?" "No, nothing. We'll see what happens when school starts again." Magdalena spoke in a soft voice, in those low but fine-tuned notes that only she was able to modulate, and Mallarino desired her again; he allowed himself to cast a direct glance at her breasts, remember them fleetingly, letting his eyes show that memory; Magdalena pretended not to notice, although women always noticed those things, and didn't fold her arms, and her face showed no sign of being uncomfortable. She said good-bye affectionately, stroking Mallarino's left arm, and he was left alone with his daughter in his new house. This was an unprecedented kind of solitude for him at that moment: he was fascinated by the novelty of the feeling, undoubtedly related to the instinctive anxiety at having sole responsibility for Beatriz and her well-being, at least for the next forty-eight hours (a vertiginous figure). This emotion brought tears to his eyes: he felt ridiculous, mocked himself. In the mists of those new impressions he thought of Cuéllar and Cuéllar's sons, whom he'd never seen, and in his mind he imagined, vivid and mobile and bright, like a film, a scene of a fistfight in a school playground, and he could almost see clothes tearing against pavement, bruises on faces, dark blood and tears, and he could almost hear the sound of the blows, bones colliding with bones. But the scene soon vanished, because Beatriz, with an irresistible smile of enthusiasm, had pulled out an old deck of cards with battered corners from her little pink knapsack and was now asking her father to play *manotón*, in spite of the fact that he'd explained to her countless times that playing the game with just two was no fun at all.

At the end of August, when classes resumed, Beatriz brought home the news (it wasn't so much news as a casual mention, an offhand comment) that Samanta Leal wasn't there anymore. She didn't mention her again. So, with dismissive ease, the girl disappeared from Beatriz's memory and perhaps that of the whole school, and Mallarino thought that he too, finding himself in the same situation, would have done the same: created a void of silence around the child, a closed and hermetic oblivion where what had happened, in not existing in the memories of those around her, would soon stop existing in her own memory. Change schools, change neighborhoods, change cities, change something, keep changing, change to leave behind, change to erase: a true pentimento, the correction to a canvas after a change of heart, an image painted over another, a brushstroke of oil paint on top of other brushstrokes. That perhaps was what had happened in the case of Samanta Leal, because oil paint cannot be erased but can be corrected; not eliminated but buried under new layers. It was easy to correct a child's life: just a couple of radical decisions and a real will, a real commitment to the correction, and that was all. Samanta Leal's parents had decided to do that, and that was to be respected; Mallarino talked about it once with Magdalena, and Magdalena agreed. As the weeks went by, and the months, Samanta Leal also began to disappear from their memories, and what should have surprised them, but didn't, was not remembering her even when they talked about what was happening to Adolfo Cuéllar.

First there were rumors. "The Witches' Post," the gossip section of a weekly magazine, ran a story about how Cuéllar and his wife had been at the center of a small scandal in the line outside a movie theater on Sixty-third Street. Later, *El Tiempo* published in its women's section—the word WOMEN headed the page in hollow letters, barely an outline—a half-page interview in which the congressman's wife spoke with pleasure about charity bazaars, literacy drives, and donations to food banks and blood banks, and Mallarino was sure he was not the only one surprised or puzzled by the omission of any mention of Adolfo Cuéllar, whose influence, direct or indirect, had made the donations and drives and bazaars possible. "Señora Cuéllar," read the text, "preferred discreetly that we not talk about her husband. 'Dirty laundry gets washed at home,' she told us." And then, one November morning, Mallarino was woken by the telephone ringing. "They've asked for his resignation," said Rodrigo Valencia from the other end of the line. "Nobody's talking about it as a punishment, because there's nothing to punish. But my spies have very clear opinions. You don't have to be too savvy to realize." It was still very early: Mallarino cradled the receiver between his shoulder and head while his hands, tingling with sleep, felt around for his cigarettes and lighter in the methodical messiness of his bedside table. "Realize what?" said Mallarino. "Well, Javier, you know," said Valencia. "Or rather, the less said the better. Watch the news tonight, I'm sure there'll be something." And there was: that night Mallarino turned on the television a couple of minutes before seven and listened with half an ear to the end of an episode of *The Mary Tyler Moore Show* while filing away the press clippings he hadn't used that week. He had time to go outside and find the dogs' plastic dishes, serve them a scoop of dog food, come back up, and wash his hands before the newscast began. The first commercial break suggested that on a salary of fifteen thousand pesos he could be a banker, asked him to drink a grape-flavored soda pop (only because a roller-skating girl was carrying one), and urgently ordered him to buy the book *The World Challenge*. After all that, the presenter's talking moustache announced the news.

The images, it seemed, had been filmed that very morning. There was Cuéllar, his head among a bed of microphones like the head of John the Baptist on Salome's platter, announcing his temporary retirement from the Congress of the Republic on the very steps of the Capitolio Nacional. "No, gentlemen, it is not a matter of trying to hush anything up," he said, replying to a question that hadn't been broadcast. That's how the news item began— with that irritated stress the voice makes in denial. "No, not at all. The reasons are personal. I'm going to take a little break, this job wears a man down, you know what I mean? My family needs me, and the family is the top priority, isn't it? At least I've always said so." Mallarino saw the image from the edge of his bed; he tried to capture, in his sketchbook with its black covers, two or three details: the nose enlarged by the cameras, the gleam of the flashes reflecting off the slicked-over hair, the high collar of the checked shirt that added a fold, and shadow under the chin. Something caught his attention: Some movement? A face he knew? Mallarino leaned forward. He saw a woman keeping a restrained silence behind the swarm of journalists; despite a background shot on television not being the same as a foregrounded newspaper portrait, he recognized Cuéllar's wife: the laboriously curled black hair, the sky-blue eye shadow, a sepia-toned silk scarf wrapped around her long neck. He didn't know what to make of that presence, for the woman's face was half hidden and her expression inscrutable, and he went back to focusing on the congressman. It was true that he looked tired: the weariness, at least, was not feigned. Mallarino could see it in his eyes, he thought, those eyes that seemed irritated by the lights, and he could also hear it in his voice: it was no longer that indiscreet and repugnant voice that had asked him for clemency and later that afternoon forgiveness, but it still had something in common with it. What was it?

The image of Cuéllar—his practiced indifference or confidence on the stone steps of the Capitol building—lasted a very short time, a few brief seconds, and was cut when, after the last of his indifferent and confident answers, the reporters rose up in an incomprehensible salvo of questions. The newscast went on to announce the dismantling of a conspiracy to overthrow the government in Spain, but Mallarino went on thinking about the head that was speaking among microphones and comparing it with the head that had spoken to him, drooping and humble, the afternoon of the party, and suddenly he was also thinking about the head of the woman who was observing the whole scene from the back, and then went back to thinking about the man at the party and the man on television. And then he knew, both were humiliated men. It was true that now, on television, the humiliation had been more obvious and notorious, but it was actually nothing more than an exacerbated or extreme version of the previous humiliation—or rather the previous one had been the seed, and the current one, broadcast on national television

at peak viewing hour, its full flowering. And now he focused on the wife again: the humiliation, all humiliation,
needs a witness. It doesn't exist without it: nobody is
humiliated alone; humiliation in solitude is not humiliation. Was Cuéllar's wife the witness at this moment? Or
were the journalists? Were the real reasons he was leaving
his post known or not? Did they or did they not have
Mallarino's drawing in mind? Did he, Adolfo Cuéllar?
What most bothered people who were caricatured, Mallarino had discovered over the years, was not seeing themselves with their defects but having everyone else see them:
as when a secret comes to light; as if their bones were a
well-guarded secret and Mallarino had all of a sudden revealed them. Did that happen to Cuéllar? His wife was
looking at him, the journalists were looking at him, Mallarino was looking at him, millions of people all over the
country were looking at him. . . . Cuéllar had become a
visible being—too visible. Mallarino imagined himself observing the city from on high and at the same time imagined the satisfaction the little people must feel, the men
and women who were too small and insignificant to be
seen by him and those like him. Perhaps Cuéllar, in these
moments, would have preferred to be one of those men
nobody sees, an anonymous and hidden creature. Or perhaps he was justly turning into one of them: by giving up
his privileged position, going into the shadows to blend in

with those who were not privileged, he was also fleeing future humiliations. Without privileges, Adolfo Cuéllar would be safe from those, like Mallarino, who see the world through the humiliations of others; those who seek out weaknesses in others—bones, cartilage—and pounce to exploit them, the way dogs smell fear. Mallarino turned off the television. As the back of his hand passed in front of the screen, he felt the tickle of static electricity on the hairs of his fingers and on his skin.

"Poor bastard," Mallarino said to the black screen, the chest of drawers, the closed blinds. "He should have just stayed home."

The second Sunday of December, just before the end-of-the-year festivities got under way in the agitated and warm city, Mallarino invited Magdalena to the first bull-fight of the season. A young Colombian torero was going to graduate to full standing; his sponsors would be two Spanish bullfighters, and one of them, Antoñete, always put on a good performance at the Santamaría Bullring; Mallarino thought that all this could provide him with the perfect pretext to spend an afternoon with his wife, just the two of them on their own, and discover if the impression he'd had lately was illusory. He'd been feeling it for days now, each time he met with Magdalena to hand over Beatriz like clandestine merchandise: it was something impossible to pinpoint, a sigh that seemed involuntary during a good-bye kiss on the cheek, a straightening up when Mallarino, with a hand on her waist, directed her through a door he was holding open. One night, after an obligation to attend together the birthday celebration of a mutual friend, they'd found themselves furiously desiring each other, and there was a tacit agreement between them to close their eyes and forget about everything, even what was about to happen, like someone placing a bet thinking that tomorrow he'll see what to do if he loses. It was a drunken fuck, a clumsy, cursing, colliding coupling in the darkness on a sofa with upholstery that left marks on their skin, and it was neither repeated nor even mentioned, except to say that if they weren't more careful things were going to get very complicated. But now, in the front row of the half-filled shady section, Mallarino thought that maybe it might not be impossible: that time had passed now, and with time, many things. The sunny section was full to bursting; he saw colored scarves, he saw faces wearing dark glasses, he saw the trees behind the flags and the brick tower blocks behind the trees, and Magdalena was at his side, and Beatriz was waiting for them at her grandparents' house. He liked—he'd always liked—the imminence of unpredictable danger, the threat that he felt each time the wooden doors spit forth one of those bulls with their four-hundred-fifty-kilo charge, and he was glad he was there, with Magdalena, knowing that she too liked some of it: she liked the music, the din of the *pasodobles* in the imperfect acoustics; she liked the heat of the early afternoon and the coolness of the end. Everything is good, thought Mallarino, and then the Colombian torero flourished a set of veronica passes and finished off the bull with know-how beyond his years. Mallarino was looking at Magdalena, at the way the sun reflected from the other side of the ring illuminated her face, when a banderillero was slightly gored and the whole bullring let out a howl and both Magdalena's hands flew to her mouth, her long fingers to her full lips, and Mallarino saw the liquid shine of her gaze and thought that maybe it might not be impossible, that time had passed, and with time, many things. Antoñete presented the Colombian torero with his sword and other accoutrements. Everyone applauded. The Colombian torero made an amusing bow; when he put his feet together he raised a little cloud of dust. It's fine to live and to die, thought Mallarino. He was fine, Magdalena was fine, everything was fine.

After the fifth bull, the crowd whistling as it was dragged away, leaving a trail of blood that seemed to coagulate in the sand in front of the audience's eyes, Mallarino looked up and thought someone was waving at him from an apartment on one of the top floors of the Torres del Parque. Someone was moving his arms, but he was far away and his face was a blurry oval, and Mallarino decided

he was waving at someone else. As he looked down, however, he saw another pair of arms, waving more exaggerat-
edly: it was Rodrigo Valencia, who was taking off his cap
as if his signals would be more comprehensible if it was in
his hand. Mallarino understood they'd see him afterward.
"Oh, look," said Magdalena. "I wonder what he's doing
here." The Valencia family had season tickets to the bull-
fights every year, as Magdalena knew very well; her sarcasm, however, did not seem to refer to that. What new
note was there in her voice? Something like resentment,
but doubtful and lukewarm, lacking conviction, the lilt of
a spoiled little girl, lurked in the air as if she and Mallarino
weren't in a public place but in the privacy of her room.
"What's wrong?" asked Mallarino. "Don't you want us to
see Valencia?" "He's going to invite us somewhere. I don't
want to do anything this evening. I wanted . . . I don't want
to do anything." "Well, I'll say no. I'll just say no to whatever he proposes. Nothing easier." Magdalena shrugged at
the same time that the sixth bull burst cheerfully out, stir-
ring up the sand with the drumroll of his hoofs. The Colombian torero was handling his cape well, but Magdalena's
mood had darkened. Her hands busied themselves with
the belt of her coat and took refuge in her deep pockets;
from behind came the smell of tobacco, and Mallarino had
a sudden urge to smoke as well. Now the whole bullring
had started whistling at the picadors: the old man next to

them whistled, sprinkling the shoulders in front of him with saliva, and Magdalena whistled, receiving disapproving looks from a lady with dyed hair. Later, when the Colombian torero missed with his sword and disenchantment flew around the bullring like slander, Magdalena seemed to be with him again, here, regretting the loss of the ears, shouting silly patriotic cheers while a small group of enthusiasts lifted the young man onto their shoulders. "How little it takes," Mallarino said to her when they were taking tiny steps on their way out, brushing up against arms and shoulders like cows in a corral. "To get carried on people's shoulders, I mean. It's as if people do it for their own pleasure."

"Maybe they do do it for their own pleasure, silly," said Magdalena.

They were just about at Seventh Avenue when Mallarino heard some hurried steps behind them and then felt a tapping of fingers on his shoulder, on the shoulder pad of his jacket. "And where are you two going?" said Rodrigo Valencia. "Answer: Nowhere. You're coming with me." Tedium clouded Magdalena's face.

"Where?" asked Mallarino. "You know post-bullfight chitchat bores me."

"We're not going to recap the corrida, Javier."

"Lots of people talking nonsense. Lots of people who don't go to see but to be seen."

"It's nothing to do with the corrida," said Valencia, suddenly serious. "I have to tell you something."

And that's how Mallarino found out: almost by accident, in an almost private moment, in the company of the woman who was almost his wife. Valencia led him, led him and Magdalena, to a restaurant on the ground floor of the Tequendama Hotel, a cold, unpleasant place with lights that were too red and from the door of which you could see the gray concrete mouth of the tunnel that led down to the underground parking garage (which, who knows why, made Mallarino intensely uneasy). At a dark table, beside the window where the name of the restaurant shone in curved neon tubes, a small group of people waited for them: Mallarino recognized two reporters from the judicial section and greeted the rest from afar, unenthusiastically, perhaps because he already knew that enthusiasm was not welcome at this meeting. "Tell Mallarino what you told me," said Valencia, the words cast out into the air without being addressed to any of them specifically, cast out so the most interested would pick them up. The one most interested was a young woman—too big now to be wearing the braces on her teeth—who began to talk about Adolfo Cuéllar as if she'd known him her whole life. She spoke of his marital problems over the last few months, well known to all, and the fact, known only to a few, that he'd recently separated from his wife, or rather his wife had asked him to leave. She spoke of Cuéllar's health, which was not impeccable, and of the diabetes that would force him to have constant checkups for the next three years. She spoke of Cuéllar's phone call that morning, demanding an appointment with such insistence that, in spite of its being a holiday and the exceptional circumstances, the doctor had to see him. She also spoke of the routine checkup that took place in the examination room—of Cuéllar in stocking feet on the scales, Cuéllar lying down barefoot while the doctor checked his pulse beside his Achilles tendon, Cuéllar without his shirt on, taking deep breaths and coughing—and the conversation that followed the checkup right there, with the patient sitting on the examination table, shirtless and shoeless. She also spoke of the things that, according to the doctor, Cuéllar had mentioned, among them several anecdotes in which his wife and sons appeared but most of all the same recurring complaint: the irreparable loss of his reputation. She spoke of the moment the doctor had left the examining room and sat down behind his desk to find stamps and letterhead notepaper to write up and sign a prescription for antidepressants, and then she spoke of what the doctor said he heard: the unmistakable sound of a window opening and, seconds later, the screeching of cars braking suddenly and the reactions of pedestrians, which must have been very noisy, because otherwise they would not have reached so high from the sidewalk of Thirteenth Avenue. And now, after telling all that, the girl with the braces looked at her colleagues, and Mallarino understood, in the same magnificent moment, that Valencia had brought him there not just to hear the tale of Adolfo Cuéllar's suicide but also to respond to the reporters' questions, or to one single declaration followed by one single question in this improvised and almost clandestine press conference. This time too it was the little girl with braces who took charge. "Maestro Mallarino," she said (and Mallarino saw the alert spiral notebooks and pens erect over them like phalluses), "we are all in agreement, as public opinion is as well, that Congressman Cuéllar's fall from grace began with your caricature. My question, our question, is: Do you feel in any way responsible for his death?"

Public opinion, thought Mallarino. *Fall from grace.* Where did those formulaic phrases come from? Who had invented them? Who had been the first to use them?

"Of course not," he said. "No caricature is capable of such a thing."

On the way back to Beatriz's grandparents' house, the silence in the car was dense, rich, concentrated. Bogotá on a Sunday evening is a vast desolate city; if it's Christmastime and the streets are festooned with lights, there is something melancholy about it, like a party that's gone wrong. Or that was the impression of Mallarino, who didn't know why he felt Magdalena's gaze weighing on him like a judgment. If at some moment, a thousand years ago, it had been possible for the day to have ended with a sort of reconciliation (and perhaps that was why they'd left Beatriz with her grandparents: to allow for an hour or two extra and the sex that might happen in that time), that possibility seemed distant now, seemed more confused with every green light they passed as they drove north up Seventh Avenue. They had to arrive in front of the building where Magdalena had grown up, to turn off the car and sit in the dark, illuminated only by the pale street-lights, for Magdalena to tell him how terrified she was at having seen what she'd seen. "What did you see?" asked Mallarino. "I don't know what you're referring to." "Of course you do, Javier, of course you know, you know perfectly well," she said. "You absolutely realized, maybe you realized even before I did. It took me a couple of seconds, I confess. I didn't realize from one moment to the next, no, but gradually. It wasn't easy, I have to admit that too, it wasn't easy to realize. But I did realize, Javier, I realized something was not right in the air, there in that horrible restaurant that seemed full of smoke even though nobody was smoking, and I was trying to think for a moment what it might be. Until I knew. It was the look in people's eyes, the look in the eyes of those reporters and even of Rodrigo Valencia: the look of admiration. They were looking at you with admiration. The guy killed himself this morning and they were interviewing you, they had to ask you that question: but they asked it with admiration. Or with astonishment, or awe, choose the word you like best. But that's what there was in the air, that sort of fear you inspire, yes, a reverential fear. And then came the worst: when I realized that you were proud. You were proud of that question they were asking you, Javier, and who knows, maybe you were proud of something else. Here, while we're talking, with our daughter asleep a few steps away, you are proud. You're proud, and I can't understand it. You're proud, and I don't know who you are anymore. I don't know who you are, but I do know one thing: that I don't want to be here. I don't want to be with you. I don't want Beatriz to be with you. I want you far away from her and far from me. I want you far, far, far away."

THREE

On Friday morning, just after eleven, Mallarino's four-by-four snaked down toward the city along the slippery road. Rain lashed the bodywork: it was one of those Bogotá downpours that make considered conversation impossible, make drivers furrow their brows and force them to grip the steering wheel hard with both hands. The mountain rose up on their left, always menacing, always on the verge of collapsing on top of people, that mountain that seemed to pass underneath the gray ribbon of road, fall away to the right in a rough, steep slope, and crash, in the distance, miraculously converted into the blurry design of the scattered city. On the horizon, that point where the western hills were no longer green but blue, airplane lights dangled in the cloudy gray sky like an old woman's earrings.

Mallarino had slept little and badly, without ever forgetting that Samanta was there, just a few steps away, in Beatriz's old room. Samanta Leal: the woman who was no longer a little girl, the woman who could lie and put on an act in order to gain access to his house and remember (or ask him to remember, like a beggar of memories) what had happened there twenty-eight years earlier. He heard her get up in the middle of the night and go to the bathroom, inevitably heard the liquid sounds she made: the stream of her urine, the indiscreet flush, the water running to wash her hands. When the first light began to shine in his window, as the gentle agitation of the hummingbirds began, Mallarino had already been awake for a while: awake and thinking about Samanta Leal, awake and feeling sorry for her, genuinely sorry, sorry for the night of total vulnerability that his guest must be enduring. Samanta was alone, alone with those new memories she'd just acquired and that altered her entire life, everything she'd believed she'd known about herself until now, or at least shifted it slightly, enough to change the whole perspective. In a Holbein painting there is a skull you can really see only from the side, not when you look straight at it: Was something similar happening to Samanta Leal? Today she would wake up feeling like somebody else; right now she would be revisiting her dearest memories and re-examining them, not with affection this time but with suspicion. Poor thing. Mallarino had given her a towel and an extra blanket, in case she felt cold. Before retreating into Beatriz's room like someone hiding out in a cave, Samanta had told Mallarino about the night of the ceremony, what had happened, and he couldn't help thinking that she sounded as if she were talking about another person. Which, in more than one sense, was perhaps true: Samanta was now another. This woman was talking about the woman she had been just a few hours ago.

Samanta told him about her colleagues at the Misión Gaia (an environmental foundation where she'd been working for the last two years) and the admiration one of them had for the life and work of Javier Mallarino. She didn't remember who had suggested they all go downtown together, to the ceremony at the Teatro Colón where Mallarino's reputation would be enshrined for all time, but the idea sparked some enthusiasm. To witness that moment: Was it not a wonderful opportunity? She accepted the invitation, more out of curiosity than anything else, and hours later found herself sitting in an unlit box, attending the beginning of what looked set to be the most boring ceremony, wondering what she'd gotten herself into, and swearing she'd slip out the first chance she got. Then they started showing the slides. An image invaded the theater, then another, and a third; Samanta looked at them absent-mindedly, the way one looks at flames in a fireplace, and after a while she noticed that she wasn't looking so absent-mindedly anymore, that she recognized some images, that she recognized a house. She turned and said to her colleague: "I've been there." This surprise made her laugh, a silly laugh. The whole situation had something absurd about it, and the smile that appeared on her colleague's face was also absurd: "You've been to Javier Mallarino's house?" And she assured him that she had been there, to that house, and he teased her and they laughed. But then Samanta began to recognize things: a couple of pictures, for example. The one with the three faces, for example. Now the whole thing didn't seem so funny. "I've seen that picture before," she told her colleague, and the irritated people sitting behind them clicked their tongues to order silence. "I've been in that house," Samanta continued, but not laughing anymore; it didn't seem such a funny surprise now; the people sitting nearby kept telling her to be quiet. So Samanta didn't say anything more about it. She stopped saying she'd been there before; she stopped saying she'd seen that picture before. She kept quiet. She wrestled as best she could with the unformed questions that were pestering her. She began to imagine possibilities. And the next day she arrived at the house in the mountains, and lied, and acted, and all the time she was trying to remember and hoping for Mallarino to remember—yes, that too: for Mallarino to remember. And all for nothing.

"I don't know why it should even matter," Samanta had said. "Here I am, Señor Mallarino: I am what I am, that's not going to change. Twenty-eight years: an entire lifetime. Who does it matter to now? Maybe it's better to just leave it all as it was. Who told me to go digging around instead of leaving well enough alone? Wasn't it better for everything to stay as it had been? Wasn't I just fine the way I was, without knowing what I now know? That belongs to another lifetime, a life that has never been my life. They took it away from me. They changed it. My parents changed it for me. They gave me another one: one where there was no past. A child's past is made of plasticine, Señor Mallarino, adults can do whatever they like with it. *We can*, I mean, we can do whatever we like. That's how it was with me. A year went by, and then another, and that life from before began to recede, until it stopped existing. That little girl from before, that girl certain things happened to, went to sleep and died, Señor Mallarino. She stopped existing, like a sickly puppy. And one fine day that girl is thirty-five years old and sees a slide projection in a theater and feels something strange, something she's never felt. I didn't know that could happen. Just to be sitting there and feel these strange things. With each passing minute, with each minute, feeling even stranger. They're talking up onstage, there are speeches, but you don't hear them. Your attention is elsewhere. You're remembering things. You have intuitions, shall we say, uncomfortable intuitions. Half-formed memories arrive, like phantoms. What do you do with this? What do you do with phantoms? That's what I've been asking myself all this time. I've begun to remember things, but now I don't know if I'm remembering because I remember, Señor Mallarino, or if I'm remembering because you told me. Am I remembering because you put the memory in my head? It's not easy, it's not easy to know. The problem is that a whole lifetime has gone by, Señor Mallarino, and my question is: Who can all this matter to? What happened, what didn't happen, who does it matter to?"

Who does it matter to, thought Mallarino this morning. He waited for the coffeepot to stop bubbling and took out the glass mug; a drop fell onto the hot stovetop and hissed like an aggressive cat. With his cup of fresh coffee in hand, Mallarino picked up the newspaper and read it standing up at the kitchen counter, his back to the frosted window, freezing to death with his charcoal pencil in hand, until he realized he wasn't taking anything in, that his mind was elsewhere. Elsewhere, yes, or in another time, and in any case far away from the newspaper—that vulgar flatterer of

the present moment—and its announcements of parties
and acts and speeches and more speeches and skies covered
in balloons, big colored balloons, all designed to celebrate
the bicentennial of Colombian independence. *Who does it
matter to,* thought Mallarino, and then: *It matters to me.*
He poured himself more coffee; he went up to his studio;
he looked at Daumier's caricature where King Louis
Philippe's same chubby face (his pear face, as Frenchmen
of the time saw him, a king with the face of a pear) looked
at the past, the present, and the future: Mallarino said to
himself that his own situation didn't seem very different at
this moment. That face was like his, perhaps. But that face
said to him: *All is the present.* What I remember, thought
Mallarino, is happening now. It was too early to call Rodrigo Valencia, so Mallarino took a sheet of paper out of
the fax machine—those too white, too thick sheets whose
edges inflicted painful paper cuts on the unwary—and
wrote a message by hand, in his careful handwriting, dat-
ing it in one corner and signing it at the end as he always
did, as if it were a letter. Valencia, he thought, would find
the message as soon as he arrived at the office.

> *Rodrigo:*
> *I want to ask you for an urgent favor. Do you
> remember Adolfo Cuéllar, the congressman? Well,*

I need his widow's details. Address, phone number,
whatever you can find for me. I don't know if I
already said it's urgent.

Very best,
Javier

The call came sooner than expected. "Well, if it isn't
the most brilliant star in the Colombian firmament," Valencia said, "and my number-one fax correspondent. Let's
see, let's see, tell me what on earth this is about. What have
you got in mind?" Mallarino thought Valencia was talking
far too loudly; for a second he was tempted to tell him to
keep his voice down, but he didn't. He asked him to remember the afternoon of the party, twenty-eight years ago,
to remember the girl, Beatriz's little friend. "She needs to
talk to Cuéllar's wife," said Mallarino, "to ask her some
things. Can you get me an address, a phone number? Ask
someone there, your secretary, one of your researchers.
Five minutes: I'm sure it wouldn't take your people any
more than five minutes." There was a silence. Mallarino
imagined Valencia's vacant stare landing anywhere: on a
pencil, his computer keyboard, the walls where caricatures
of him and his wife that Mallarino had drawn years ago
hung. Finally, Valencia said: "That girl? You know the
girl?"

"Look, it's a long story," said Mallarino. "She's here, with me, and needs that information."

"Just a moment, one moment. She's with you?"

"Will you get it for me or not?"

"One moment, Javier. For you, or for the girl? Who must not be a girl anymore, but anyway. What is this about her being there with you? What's her name?"

"Will you get me the information?"

"What's her name?"

"Samanta Leal. What does it matter to you? Will you get me the information?"

"But I just don't understand. I need more details, there's something missing. No, I know what I'm missing: understanding. I don't understand, that's what's wrong."

"You don't have to understand, Rodrigo: you just have to do me a favor. And doing favors is easier than understanding. Look, it's very simple. You're in your office, right? There in that glass case you have instead of an office, in everyone's sight. So follow my instructions. Raise your hand, so they see you from outside. When the first of your slaves comes in, you ask him to do this. And when you have it, send me a fax. So very simple."

"But what for?" asked Valencia. "How did that person get to your house? What is she asking you for? What's going on, that's what I want to know."

"Nothing's going on."

"Of course it is. Either tell me, Javier, or I'm not help-ing you."

"Then don't help me," said Mallarino. "And go to hell."

"Look, Javier, try to see it from my point of view," said Valencia. "This is not normal. Or do you think it is? Does it seem normal to you for that girl to appear just like that?"

"She's not a girl."

"For her to appear so many years later and ask you for this?"

"She hasn't asked me for anything," said Mallarino. "This idea is mine."

"How's that?"

"It's to help her. She doesn't remember."

Mallarino then remained in the company of the silence of the phone line, that imperfect silence, like darkness for blind people. In his imagination, Valencia was one of those nineteenth-century caricatures where the person appears covered in question marks and with an intense expression of confusion, and then he imagined Valencia's head con-verted into a silhouette, a black line, and those three words, *She doesn't remember*, banging against the line, desperate flies in a glass box. After a long few seconds, longer still because over the phone time cannot be measured on the features of one's interlocutor—one doesn't notice the barely perceptible changes, the warnings, the intentions sketched across them—Valencia grunted a couple of times, something like a clearing of the throat, like a contained belch. "Ah," he said then, "I see what's going on. The girl doesn't know."

"She's not a girl," said Mallarino.

"She doesn't know, that's the problem. She was never told."

"She doesn't remember."

"And you want to help her."

"Help her to remember."

"Help her to find out," said Valencia, as if he were spitting out a caramel he was choking on. "Because if she doesn't know, then neither do you."

Something resembling relief: that's what Mallarino felt. Perhaps because someone else, not him, had said what he didn't dare say. *Because if she doesn't know, then neither do you:* Was it not incredible, and also fascinating, that they were talking about the past? What was not known now—now that Rodrigo Valencia mentioned it—was something that in the past had been known, something about which there had been certainty at some point; so certain had Mallarino been that he'd drawn a cartoon about it. Was what appeared in the press not true beyond all doubt or uncertainty? Was a page in the newspaper not the supreme proof that something had happened? Mallarino imagined the past as a watery creature with imprecise contours, a sort of deceitful, dishonest amoeba that can't be

investigated because, looking for it again under the micro-
scope, we find that it's not there, and we suspect that it's
gone, but we soon realize it has changed shape and is now
impossible to recognize. *Because if she doesn't know, then
neither do you.* So certainties acquired at some moment in
the past could, in time, stop being certainties: something
could happen, a fortuitous or deliberate event, and suddenly all evidence is invalidated, the truth ceases to be true,
the seen ceases to have been seen, and the occurrence to
have occurred; all lose their place in time and space, are
devoured and passed on to another world, or to another
dimension of our world, a dimension we don't know. But
where is it? Where does the past go when it changes? In
which folds of our world are they hiding, cowardly and
ashamed, the events that had been unable to remain, to
keep being true in spite of the wear and tear of time, to
win their place in human history? *Because if she doesn't
know, then neither do you.* But the problem with Samanta
Leal wasn't that she didn't know, it was that she didn't
remember: that memory, her childhood memory, had
suffered certain distortions, certain—how to put it—
interferences. It was a question of restoring it: for this and
no other reason, they needed to speak with Cuéllar's
widow, ask her a couple of simple questions, get a couple of
simple answers. "It's not for me," said Mallarino. "It's for
her. I want to help her."

"But have you thought this through, Javier?" asked Valencia.

"There's not much to think through."

"Have you thought about the consequences? Don't tell me there won't be any consequences. Don't tell me you haven't imagined them. Let's see, let me see: The girl remembers nothing?"

"She's not a girl. And no, she doesn't remember anything."

"I see. For her it's as if nothing had happened."

"Exactly."

"Except that it did happen, Javier."

Mallarino said nothing.

"It did happen," said Valencia, "and we all saw it."

What strange arrogance moved, like the undertow near the shore, beneath those apparently simple words, so vague, so everyday. The arrogance was to simulate or even covet those certainties, as if Valencia could now be sure of not only what he himself saw but what others saw, others who, twenty-eight years later, were absent or gone or, in any case, silent. The memory of others: how much he would gladly pay at this moment for a ticket to that spectacle! There, thought Mallarino, lay the origin of our dissatisfaction and sadness: the impossibility of sharing memory with others.

"But that doesn't matter," said Mallarino. "At least, that

doesn't matter to me. It's her. The poor thing has a right to know."

"Oh, it's just for her."

"That's what I'm trying to tell you."

"Just for her, yeah," said Valencia. "What do you take me for, an idiot?"

Mallarino said nothing.

"You think I don't realize?" said Valencia. "Well, I do realize. I see perfectly well. What might happen now if nothing happened that night. What could change for you. And I understand, believe me, I understand your worry, at least in principle."

"I'm not worried."

"I think you are. Because if nothing happened, and you did that drawing . . . Of course, of course I understand. But can I tell you something? We were all there. And can I tell you something else? The last thing you want to do is to start asking questions. That's the last. You're not guilty of anything, Javier."

"But who's talking about guilt?" Mallarino cut him off. "I'm not talking about guilt, nobody's talking about guilt. I'll tell you one more time, Rodrigo: It's not for me. It's for her."

Silence. A moment later, when Valencia spoke, it was as if his voice had fallen to the floor: a stepped-on, worn-out, used-up voice.

"I see," he said. "And so the idea is to find the widow."

"Yes."

"And speak to her, ask her."

"Yes."

"But how stupid," Valencia said wearily. "That's the stupidest thing I've ever heard in my life."

"I don't see why," said Mallarino. "We just . . ."

"What idiots," said Valencia.

"Hey, just a minute."

"What an idiot you are. I won't say anything about her, I don't know what's in her head. But you're an idiot. And what are you going to do, if you don't mind my asking?"

"I don't know what we're going to do. But that's something . . ."

"You're going to knock on her door and she's going to invite you in, *How are you, how's it going,* and is she going to offer you a coffee? Or is the girl going to introduce herself: *Pleased to meet you, señora, I'd like to know what it was your husband did to me.* Is that it?"

"Go to hell, Valencia."

"No, that's not it, is it? That's not it. She's the least of it, Javier, what matters least to you is what happened to her. You want to confirm that you didn't make a mistake, isn't that it? You want to be convinced. It's idiotic, Javier, think it through, you have to see. We were all there. All of us, we were all there: Are you going to cast doubt on what happened, when all of us were there? But let's suppose it didn't, suppose that didn't happen. Tell me, what do you want to change? It can't be changed now, Javier, that's all done and finished. Cuéllar jumped from the fifth story of a building: nothing more irreversible than that. And can I tell you something? No one's missing him. We haven't missed him in all these years. We're better off without him. More than that: we've all forgotten him. He's forgotten. The country forgot him. Even his party forgot him. Back then they were ashamed of him, Javier, you think anyone's interested in his name appearing in the newspapers again? He was a despicable guy, that Cuéllar. You, on the other hand, are important: you're important to the newspaper and important to the country. This country is a jungle, Javier. We count on a few people to help us get to the other side, safe and sound, without being devoured by savage beasts. And the beasts are everywhere. You look up and you realize. Everywhere, Javier. And they're disguised, they're where you least expect them. Let's say you were mistaken. Let's say we were mistaken. In any case, the guy was despicable. He'd demonstrated it a thousand times, he would have demonstrated it a thousand more. Now you're going to turn him into a martyr, even if only for his widow? You're going to go and confess that you did that drawing without really having seen, without really being sure. Very well.

And then what? Can you imagine what the beasts could do with that? Can you imagine what will happen when the beasts realize they can cut your head off? And for something that happened so long ago, besides. Do you think they're going to spare you? Well, they're not. They're going to cut off your head, the beasts of this beastly country are going to cut your head off. Everyone who hates you, who hates us, all the fanatics are going to go for your jugular. When they realize that you have doubts, that you're not sure anymore, they're going to be all over you. No one can afford doubt these days, Javier. This is not a world for doubters. You have to look tough, because if you don't, you'll get killed. You want to stand in front of them, take off your bulletproof vest, and tell them to fire. And they're going to fire, believe me. They're going to shoot you. What good is that, Javier? Tell me, explain it to me, explain the utility of this whole ridiculous thing, because I can't see any, I swear by my fucking mother I can't see it. I don't know what good this is going to do and I need you to tell me. Clearly, without any stupid metaphors, without any nonsense. Tell me, tell me in two words: What good is it going to do?"

"None for you," said Mallarino. "But it might do her some good."

Silence.

"To hell with you, Javier," said Valencia. "To hell with you both."

And he hung up.

So what he could have found out in twenty minutes he ended up finding out in two hours: Mallarino had to get out his yellowing address book, which was falling apart, poor mangy little thing, and call a court reporter and some journalists for the competition—the national, news, and police desks—and even a member of congress who owed him several favors. In a few minutes they were calling him back, each and every one of them, bending over backward to meet Javier Mallarino's immediate needs. His name helped, he had to admit, but he was not the least bit concerned about exploiting his reputation to achieve these modest ends, for, after all, were not these journalists and politicians the ones who had given him this reputation and the power that went with it? One thing was sure: Mallarino would have gotten the information much more quickly had the people he asked been in possession of it. But they weren't: some of them had a hard time remembering Cuéllar; others didn't even know he'd ever existed. Valencia was right: the man had been swallowed up by oblivion. Not surprising in this amnesiac country obsessed with the present, this narcissistic country where not even the dead

are capable of burying their dead. Forgetfulness was the
only democratic thing in Colombia: it covered them all,
the good and the bad, the murderers and the heroes, like
the snow in the James Joyce story, falling upon all of them
alike. Right now there were people all over Colombia
working hard to have certain things forgotten—small
or big crimes, or embezzlements, or tortuous lies—and
Mallarino could bet that all of them, without exception,
would be successful in their endeavor. Ricardo Rendón
had also been forgotten. Not even he had managed to be
saved. Maybe Rodrigo Valencia had also been right about
that: it was no use. *What good is it going to do?* he'd asked,
and he meant something else, of course, but he'd managed
to get Mallarino to retain the question and ask himself
now, with some melancholy: What good is it going to do?

And now his four-by-four was entering the city, and
the mountain road turned gradually into a suburban road
and then the avenue, and the rain clouds seemed to pass
them going the other way, stubbornly returning to where
they'd come from: the house in the mountains. Mallarino
detested this stretch where one found oneself suddenly surrounded by horrendous brick buildings, the temperature
went up two or three degrees, and drivers, caught un-
awares by the change, began, in risky maneuvers, to take
their jackets off while driving. He had never had to take
his jacket off: unlike most of the people who lived in the

mountains, who left their houses all wrapped up in over-
coats and scarves (it was not unusual to see someone driving in leather gloves), Mallarino tended to dress in light
clothes, no more than a shirt and corduroy blazer that
changed color when he brushed it with his hand, and preferred to leave his raincoat on the backseat of the car,
ready for any eventuality. Samanta Leal, sitting beside
him, had complained of the cold and ducked her head between her shoulders, like a chick, and had only recently
started to relax. The sheet with the information was a tube
of coiled paper; the woman's hands gripped the tube as if
she were pushing a lawn mower. Mallarino looked at them
out of the corner of his eye, looked at the white knuckles
and the delicate ring that was their only adornment, and
then looked at Samanta's profile: the strong angle of her
jaw; the shoulders of an attentive student, pressed against
the back of the seat; the seat belt that crossed between her
breasts like a hunter's quiver. There, in the roll of paper,
were the address and telephone number of Carmenza de
Torres, who was once the wife of Adolfo Cuéllar and was
the mother of his sons and then was his widow; Carmenza
de Torres, who found herself obliged, after the death of
her husband the congressman, to complete her studies in
hostelry and tourism, which she'd given up at the time of
her first pregnancy, and eventually ended up working at a

travel agency, distinguishing herself in sales, becoming the owner's personal assistant, marrying him, and starting a new life with a new surname: a clean surname, a surname without memories. All this Mallarino found out with the help of his admirers. He also found out that the agency was called Unicorn Travels, and that the office was located across from the Parque Nacional, and that Doña Carmenza went there every afternoon, from two till six, but never in the morning ("*Every* afternoon?" Mallarino had asked; "Yes, *every* afternoon," he was assured). Now, driving toward the ring road at forty kilometers an hour, Mallarino outlined the day's itinerary for Samanta. He'd drop her off at her house so she could rest a little and change her clothes; he'd keep an appointment he had downtown; they'd meet at the travel agency at three o'clock. Did that seem good to Samanta? She, staring straight ahead, nodded the way a condemned prisoner might nod

An appointment downtown. What would Magdalena be doing right now? He suddenly felt an urgent need to see her, to be with her and hear her voice, as if by doing so he could prove in some twisted way that not all the past was changeable and unstable. Magdalena was also the past. But Magdalena was firm. Mallarino imagined her, by some sort of automatism, in front of a double microphone, two long silvery tubes. The desk in the image was made of wood and covered in a brown cloth; on top of the cloth was a stopwatch, so Magdalena could time her monologues without consulting the digital clock on the wall. But all this was mere speculation: he wasn't even sure that Magdalena recorded her programs in the morning. On the avenue, the traffic was moving slowly, more slowly than usual. The four-by-four passed between unfinished rust-colored buildings and urban trees, those sad trees with their crowns that nobody ever sees and their asphyxiated leaves on the lower branches. Samanta had given directions and proposed the best routes, drawing a map with words that Mallarino could imagine in his head, and then she had gone quiet, as if hoping the silence would be strong enough to make Mallarino forget her presence. "Where should I turn off?" he asked. Her hand moved in front of the windshield, incomplete shadow of a little dove, but not a word came from her mouth, and when he turned his head, trying all the time to keep an eye on the traffic, Mallarino realized that Samanta had started to cry. They were stealthy and weary tears, like those of someone who has already cried a lot: these were remainders, leftover tears. "Don't cry, Samanta," he said; he felt immediately, irrevocably stupid, but searching through the archives of his head, he could find no other consoling words. He didn't have very many to begin with, and he didn't often use them. And he felt immediately, irrevocably stupid.

"I'm sorry," said Samanta. She smiled, wiped both eyes with the same hand, smiled again. "It's just that I was fine. I didn't need this."

"I know," said Mallarino.

"Can I ask you something?"

"Ask away."

"What happens now?"

"What do you mean?"

"Well, just that: What happens now? Or rather: What's going to happen this afternoon? What's going to happen after three? Am I obliged to carry on as before? I don't know what I'm going to be told, but do I have that obligation? And what if I decide I don't want to, that I don't want any of this? Right now, here, before we get to my house. What happens if I'd rather forget all this again? What if I'd rather go back to how things were before that fucking ceremony? Don't I have that right?"

"Is that what you want, Samanta?"

"Oh, I don't know," she said. "I have a headache."

"We can stop and buy something."

"And I want to change my clothes," said Samanta. "I can't stand wearing dirty clothes."

"Well, those dirty clothes look very good on you," said Mallarino. He hadn't meant it to sound like a cheap flirtatious compliment but that's how the words came out. Not that it wasn't true: in the morning, when he saw Samanta

emerge from Beatriz's old room with her hair wet from
the shower but wearing the same blouse and the same
skirt from the day before, Mallarino had found the entire
scene strangely erotic. He didn't say so to Samanta, of
course: women have no reason to comprehend men's idiotic impulses, or even put up with or tolerate them, or en-
dure every compliment thrown at them, no matter how
well intentioned. That's what his had been, but nevertheless he noticed, or thought he noticed, a sudden tension in
Samanta's muscles, her shoulders bracing against the back
of her seat, her stretched-out legs folding up. Had it bothered her? "I have a headache," she said again, but talking
to herself this time. A motorcycle with its light on veered
past; behind them was a pickup truck with darkened windows and, farther back, a military van with rifle barrels
sticking out: the president, or some minister? Now Samanta wiped her eyes again, rubbing them carelessly, the
way you're never supposed to do (a risk of seriously scratch-
ing the corneas). On her index finger, Mallarino noticed a
wet trail like that of a snail. "Where should I turn?" said
Mallarino.

"Pretty soon," said Samanta, "I'll let you know." And
after a silence: "This is fucking hell. Not knowing is not
hell. The hellish thing is not knowing whether I want to
know. Or if I'm better off the way I was before." Mallarino said yes, that he felt the uncertainty too, that he

also— "No, you don't know," Samanta cut him off. Mallarino sensed some hostility. "You can't know. None of you
can. People like you think you know, imagine you know,
and it's not true. If you only knew how insulting that is.
Believing you know. Believing you can imagine. It's not
like that."

"You don't understand, Samanta."

"It's an insult. That you believe. That you imagine."

"That's not what I meant to say," said Mallarino. "Don't
be like this, please."

With a gesture that struck Mallarino as both weak and
at the same time authoritarian, Samanta pointed to a street
with dark brick walls topped with broken glass: some
transparent, some green, testimony to other, more inno-
cent times when such strategies deterred thieves. "Turn
down here. Then take the second right. But don't miss it,
or it'll take forever to get back around." Samanta's voice
sounded fragile, as if it were catching somewhere. "That
building, the only one there is," she said, or rather ordered,
and raised her hand enough to point at a brick box with
white aluminum-framed windows and net curtains behind the windows and silhouettes of women behind the
net curtains: there, on a street of old Chapinero houses,
Samanta's building looked like something someone had
forgotten. She pointed to a spot by the curb where Mallarino could park: beside a tree with a thick trunk and roots

growing over the pavement. A car must have just left, after the rain stopped, because a perfect, dry rectangle of lighter gray was still visible on the dark gray surface. Before they had stopped completely, with the wheezing murmur of the car's engine still cutting off the softest syllables, Samanta said: "Fifteen, Señor Mallarino." A bicycle messenger went past, his right trouser leg tucked inside a fluorescent orange sock. "I was fifteen years old. My dad was away on a trip. He traveled a lot—an insurance salesman can travel a lot: Cali, Cartagena, Medellín, and at some point Caracas, Quito, Panama. I was at a party. My mother asked me specifically to come home early, because my dad was arriving home from a trip that night and we had to be home waiting for him. My mother's life revolved around things like that. Having his dinner ready. His family waiting for him when he got home. I was a good girl, did what I was told. And that night, when I got home, I found my mother waiting in the kitchen. All the lights in the house were turned off, except for the one on the stove. You know the one? The little yellow light on the extractor fan, which was on even though nothing was cooking. And my mother there, sitting by the counter, eating fried pork rinds out of the bag. That's something I'll never forget: the crackling; pork rinds right out of the package. She told me he hadn't come home. At six the next morning we drove across the city, went into the airport parking lot. He always left his

car at the airport: his trips lasted two days, never any longer. We went into the parking lot and drove around for a
long time, until we found it. There was my dad's car. I
looked through the window to see what was inside. I don't
know what I expected to find, but I looked in. The windows were dirty, because it had rained. And do you know
what I saw, Señor Mallarino?" He gripped an imaginary
bar; he waited for a terrifying or macabre revelation. "I
didn't see anything," said Samanta. "There was nothing
inside. Not a keychain, not a single toll receipt, no loose
change. The windows dirty and the car, inside, clean.
Clean as if he were going to sell it that afternoon. I think
my mother knew deep down. She didn't seem worried: I
thought that deep down she knew my dad had left . . . and
the weird thing is that none of this has ever been a problem for me, Señor Mallarino. What happened to my family has happened to hundreds of families, thousands. For
me it's never been a problem. But last night I began to ask
myself stupid things. What did my dad's leaving have to do
with that night? Was there any link? No, what link could
there be, I don't see it. But is there one, even though I can't
see it?" Mallarino saw her press her jaw to her chest,
squeeze her eyes shut. "What I want to know is what happened here," Samanta said then. Her voice, damp and
thick, had a sort of urgency in the rarefied air inside the
car. "Here," said Samanta. She began to cry again, but her

crying was more candid this time; it distorted her features, stole her beauty. Samanta was patting her belly and mouth, the expression on her mouth stretched. "What happened here," she was saying, "I want to know what happened here." Mallarino stared at her hands; he interrogated them, interrogated their tapping against her body; Mallarino didn't understand. There, parked in front of her building, Samanta grimaced with impatience and her mouth suddenly released a pent-up breath.

It was a rapid movement: she put both feet up on the dashboard and lifted up her hips and pulled her green wool tights and her soft white underpants down with a single skillful shove, sticking both thumbs under the elastic, under both elastic waistbands at once, and pushing forward, not in a straight line but tracing a curve in the air like a bowl, like a smile. The mess of wrinkled clothes bunched around her ankles, and in a brief instant Mallarino saw the calves covered with clusters of red spots and a violet oval on one thigh, where she had a bruise. Samanta separated her knees, opening her legs, and all the light in the world invaded the four-by-four and illuminated the pale sex, straight, blond, sparse pubic hairs, the insolent vulva. Samanta's hand closed over her vulva, moved away, then closed again with straight fingers over the diaphanous skin of her lips: "Here," said Samanta, "I want to know what happened here. Is this what you saw, Señor

Mallarino? Was this what you saw twenty-eight years ago? What do you think? Has it changed a lot?" Mallarino looked up and saw, in a window of the brick building, the silhouette of someone who'd pulled aside the net curtains to get a better view. No, it wasn't a curious man, not a Peeping Tom: it was an older woman, and Mallarino managed to see her housecoat and her expression of revulsion before she hid behind the delicate white shadows of the curtains. He tried to turn around; he was prevented from doing so by his seat belt; Mallarino unfastened it and turned around to reach for his raincoat on the backseat. He found it on the floor (it must have slipped off the seat on the way down the mountain road) and grabbed it with one hand and threw it on top of Samanta, at first with irritated gestures, and then as if covering up a little girl with a chill. "Here, here, here," she was saying, and she covered her face with her hands. Mallarino, without knowing why, began to address her familiarly. "There, there," he said. "Get dressed. Everything's going to be okay."

She sat up and folded her knees to her chest, hugged her legs. "I didn't ask for this," he heard her say. "I was perfectly fine." Mallarino read the shame in her voice, and the exhaustion, and the bitterness, and the terrible vulnerability.

"Everything's going to be fine," he told her. He stroked her hair. He desired her, and detested himself for desiring her. He looked toward the doorman's booth to see whether the doorman had noticed anything. On the gray tree trunk somebody had engraved, with a knife, two names and a heart. PAHY, he read, before realizing that it wasn't an H but two T's crossed with the same horizontal stroke.

"Get dressed," he said to Samanta. "Go upstairs, get a bit of sleep. I'll see you at three."

Magdalena thought that having lunch there, a few steps away from the Matisse and Giacometti and Klimt drawings, would be exciting for Mallarino: to judge from his reputation as an anchorite, as an old sage hidden in the mountains, he no longer frequented the neighborhood of La Candelaria as much as he used to, in the old days, much less this museum, which still today, ten years after opening, shone as if it were brand-new. Magdalena had called that morning and reserved a table on the patio in the courtyard, but now she regretted it; after the rain, the Bogotá sky had cleared as if a curtain had fallen away, and now the midday light shone brightly on the high white walls, the aluminum tables, the paper placemats, and it blinded the diners. The two of them had walked there from Fifth Avenue, while she told him about the program she'd recorded the previous afternoon and he complained about the filthy smells: the fried-food stands reusing the same oil over and over again, but also the street dogs, the homeless people's blankets beside building entrances, and also the shit, the shit that appeared by surprise on the corners, the origin of which it was best not to imagine. That assault on his senses contrasted sharply with the memory, still recent and raw, of what had happened with Samanta Leal. He mustn't talk about that. He had to keep it to one side: there, in another world, in an alternate world with incomprehensible rules. As they came in through the Eleventh Street entrance, up the tall step, and around Botero's dark bronze hand, Mallarino had already made the decision not to talk about what he'd seen and heard back in the house in the mountains since the last time he was with Magdalena. One day had gone by, not much more than a day: yet centuries and centuries had come and gone. Now the sun was shining on the white walls and dazzling them, and the waiter had brought a bottle of white wine, but white wine was not white but golden: wine is sunlight held together by water. Where had he heard that before? Maybe Magdalena would remember, she was good at things like that. Now she was pouring the wine, and enjoying doing so; her short haircut suited her strong-boned face, her cheeks straight out of a Pre-Raphaelite painting, her nose descending from her eyebrows in a long, elegant line. Trying all the time to keep at bay the bothersome images, the interfering words, he thought of Samanta Leal. If he didn't mention her, if he didn't mention the last few hours or the three p.m. appointment, maybe this time in Magdalena's company could turn into a necessary and urgent moment of tranquillity. Let the world stop spinning: that's all he asked. That it would stop revolving, that everyone would be quiet. Yes, let there be a little silence so he could just hear this voice that was talking to him now, this voice that was husky and smooth at the same time, the voice of a cello, one of those voices that paralyze the hand of someone about to turn a dial, that translate the chaos of the world and convert its obscure jargon into a diaphanous tongue. Interpret this world for me, Magdalena, tell me what's happening to us and what might happen now, what could happen to me now and what could happen to Samanta Leal, tell me how to remember what hasn't happened yet. And suddenly there was that phrase again that kept coming back to him, like a fiber of meat stuck in his teeth.

"'It's a poor sort of memory that only works backwards,'" recited Mallarino. "Who said that?"

Magdalena chewed a couple of times.

"The White Queen says it to Alice," she said, her mouth half full, her lively eyes smiling. "Beatriz loved that book, I don't know how many times we read it."

But Beatriz was not here. Beatriz was away on a trip, Beatriz was always away, Beatriz never stopped, perhaps out of fear of not being able to take off again if she did. The White Queen said it to Alice. Beatriz loved that book. Yes, he'd read it to her too once or twice, or at least a few pages, and he remembered having seen her—in a hammock, on holiday—reading it by herself when she was old enough to. The image of his daughter reading always moved him, perhaps because he saw on her face the same signs of intense concentration he already knew from Magdalena's face, the same arrangement of muscles between the eyebrows and around the lips, and he couldn't help but wonder about the purpose of such inherited traits, what evolutionary aim could be served by daughters making the same gestures as their mothers when a tale interested them. Beatriz loved that book: Magdalena had remembered; Magdalena always remembered. "Have you heard from her?" Mallarino asked.

"Yes. She wrote to me a couple of days ago. One piece of good news and one bad."

"Let's see," said Mallarino. "Bad news first."

"They're splitting up."

"That's the good news."

"Don't joke," said Magdalena. "She's going through a tough time, poor thing. You should be thankful they don't have kids."

"I'm thankful," said Mallarino. "So what's the good news, then?"

"She's coming to live in Colombia."

"But she already lives in Colombia."

"All right. She's staying put in Colombia."

"What does that mean?"

"She requested a transfer. I don't know what it's called, she didn't really explain. She asked not to move around all the time. She asked to stay here."

"In Bogotá?"

"No, no. In a place where she's needed, Javier. Down in Meta. Or up in Cesar."

"She doesn't know where?"

"Not yet. She knows they'll grant her the transfer, but she doesn't know where she'll be sent. She won't be in Bogotá, that's for sure. But we'll see more of her."

"How do you know?"

"Because she told me. She told me we'd see her more often. She said: 'We'll see more of each other.' She said she's been feeling lonely, that she'd been feeling lonely for months. And she would have told you the same, if you had a computer."

But Mallarino realized it wasn't a serious reproach: it was a game, a friendly wink, a dig in the ribs. Her infallible instinct told Magdalena that this was not a moment for serious reproaches. What had she noticed? How had she noticed it? Oh, but that was Magdalena: a sublime reader of reality, and especially that circumscribed and impoverished reality, that melancholy and daunted reality that was Mallarino. "Well, we'll keep her company," he said. "She's not going to be lonely here." Beatriz's husband was the youngest son of a family of conservative Catholic Popayán landowners who had a reputation, as far as Mallarino knew, of being on the wrong side since the beginning of the years of political violence. "I know more or less what that family's like," Mallarino had said to Beatriz once, "and I don't much like you going out with him." "Well, his family knows exactly who you are," answered Beatriz. "And they don't like him going out with me at all." And now, a few years after that conversation and many after her own parents' separation, Beatriz was splitting up with her husband. Juan Felipe Velasco was his name: a blond guy with a cleft chin who crossed himself every time he was about to drive somewhere. Beatriz had learned to cross herself with him, and would have taught their children to cross themselves if they'd had any; but they hadn't had any, and that was lucky; and now they were splitting up, they too were worn down by the diverse strategies that life has to wear lovers down, too many trips or too much togetherness, the accumulated weight of lies or stupidity or lack of tact or mistakes, the things said at the wrong time, with immoderate or inappropriate words, or those that, the appropriate or moderate words not having been found, were never said; or worn down too by a bad memory, yes, by the inability to remember what's essential and live within it (to remember what once made the other happy: How many lovers had succumbed to that negligent forgetting?), and by the inability, as well, to get ahead of all that wearing down and deterioration, to get ahead of the lies, the stupidity, the lack of tact, the mistakes, the things that shouldn't be said, and the silences that should be avoided: to see all that, see it all coming from way off, see it coming and step aside and feel it blow past like a meteorite grazing the planet. See it coming, thought Mallarino, and step aside. For an indigenous tribe in Paraguay, or maybe it was Bolivia, the past is what is in front of us, because we can see it and know it, but the future is what is behind, what we do not see and cannot know. The meteorite always comes from behind: we don't see it, we can't see it. You need to see it, to see it coming and step aside. You need to face the future. It's a poor sort of memory that only works backwards.

He looked around, beyond Magdalena's luminous face; and to his left, beyond the glass wall that separated the patio from the interior; and to his right, across the courtyard, toward the museum entrance. Two, three, four couples: How many would be splitting up right now? How many would be splitting up even without knowing it, heading slowly for disintegration? In the courtyard, a little boy in shorts was running after a minuscule bouncing ball. The ball was rolling toward the storm drains; the boy shouted, calling for help. And Samanta Leal? He hadn't asked her if she was married, if she had children, someone with whom to share the suffering, or at least disperse it. She was the same age as Beatriz, had the same thirty-five years they'd both had in which to achieve so many things. That's what Mallarino was thinking when someone from one of the nearby tables, a man who'd been eating on the other side of the glass, looked him in the eyes and stood up (his hands folding the napkin) and began to walk toward the open door. He waited until he was beside the table before speaking; when he did, Mallarino found the contrast between his size—and the size of the hand he extended in greeting—and his obsequious manner startling. "You are Javier Mallarino," he said, halfway between a statement and a consultation.

Magdalena looked up. Her fork remained suspended in the air. Mallarino nodded. He shook the outstretched hand.

"Thank you for your work," the man said. "I admire you, sir. I, uh, admire you very much."

"How the world has changed," said Magdalena when

the man had gone back to his chair on the other side of the glass. The scene had visibly amused her: she spoke with irony, but also with flagrant satisfaction at the corner of her mouth, turned up in her ironic smile. "This is something I've never witnessed. Since when does this happen to you?"

"Since today," said Mallarino. "Or since yesterday. But I didn't come into town yesterday."

"Can it be that people still read newspapers?"

"I suppose so."

"You could have done your *Titanic* pose," said Magdalena. "Given your fans a treat."

Mallarino smiled down at his plate. "Don't mock me."

He shifted in his chair, turning to one side and pressing his back against the cool aluminum, as if trying to get a better view of the place. Magdalena asked him if his hernia was bothering him, if he wanted them to get the bill and walk around for a while, and only then did he realize that, yes, his hernia was bothering him (a dull ache in his tailbone, his left leg already uncomfortable). Magdalena knew. How pleasant that was, and how surprising to notice the persistence of the past, the stubborn presence between them of the years of their marriage. They knew each other well, but it wasn't just that: it was, undoubtedly, having met so young, having started living together and gone

through the first disappointments and then the long march
of learning (and now they'd learned, but it was too late to
apply the lessons). All that was still present, like another
guest at the table, and that's what they owed the comfort
to, the relaxed way Magdalena set her cutlery down together on the empty plate and, just as he'd done earlier,
leaned back silently in her chair. Why had her second marriage failed? Nine years after leaving Mallarino, Magdalena had married an easygoing commercial lawyer, and
anybody would have thought—second chances are easier
to make the most of—that the relationship was definitive.
It was not: Mallarino found out vaguely about it from the
rumor mill and, once, from the Pink Telephone section of
El Tiempo, which also carried a rumor about Pablo Escobar's possible surrender. (In one of his cartoons of the time,
Mallarino had drawn Escobar alongside the victims of his
most recent terrorist attack. On one side of the box appeared the priest Rafael García Herreros, wearing his cas-
sock and saying: "Don't worry, my son. I know you're
basically a good man.") Magdalena's marriage ended in
eighteen months; Mallarino never tried to find out why.
Now he could. Did he want to? Now he could. A heavy
cloud darkened the patio; Mallarino felt a chilly breeze
and the pores of his skin closing up all of a sudden. Magdalena clenched her fists above her chest and raised her

shoulders, and Mallarino had the unmistakable feeling, as concrete as a tug in the vertebrae, that it was getting late. That's what he said to himself: *I'm running out of time,* or rather those words lit up his mind. He immediately realized, with some amazement, that he was not thinking about the hours of the day.

"Come and live with me," he said.

She stood up as if she'd been expecting the request (there was no surprise on her face—or was Mallarino reading it wrong?). Tidy girl that she was, she pushed the chair in to tuck it under the table, and the legs made an irritating metallic sound against the concrete floor.

"Let's go," she replied. "I have to get back to the studio."

They walked down a corridor to the main courtyard. They crossed it, passing beside the stone fountain that was distractedly spitting out a squalid little stream. Mallarino managed to catch a glimpse of Lucian Freud's *Blond Girl*, which he liked so much, but he immediately looked away, in case he accidentally caught sight of the study for *The Guitar Lesson*. When they came out on Eleventh Street, the sky had clouded over, the shadows disappearing from the walls, and small groups of students were gathering on the steps of the library. They went down to Seventh and turned north. Magdalena had taken Mallarino's arm. "What do you think?" he asked. "Isn't it a good idea?" It wasn't easy to walk on that crowded sidewalk, whose traffic obliged them to make themselves small, to turn sideways so another pedestrian could get past with her briefcase, or his bag of vegetables, or a child dragged by the hand and forced to walk on tiptoes. "I had hoped, my dear," said Magdalena, "that it wouldn't occur to you." They were passing in front of the marble plaques on the Agustín Nieto building, and Mallarino noticed a guy with long white hair who was copying the inscriptions, by hand, onto the pages of a notebook, or something that looked like a notebook; the guy was visible even from the other side of the street, for there, in the midst of the perilous crowds, his was the only figure that kept still. "I can't do that, Javier," said Magdalena. "I can't now. A lot of time has passed, and I have a life without you, and it's a life I enjoy. I enjoyed the other night too, of course, I enjoyed it a lot. But I like my life the way it is. It has taken me years to get it together and I like it the way it is. I like solitude, Javier. At this stage in life I've discovered that I like my solitude. Beatriz hasn't discovered it yet, but I think I can teach her. It would be a good gift, to teach my daughter how to be alone, to enjoy her solitude. I enjoy my solitude. You can understand that, I imagine. I think you can understand, can't you? I think it's too late now." Mallarino was not surprised that she used those words, almost the same ones he'd used to himself a few minutes earlier. "It's never really too late, of course, it depends on the person. But what you're proposing is not for me, it's not for us," said Magdalena. "We don't have time for this anymore." From the other side of Jiménez Avenue, at the end of the oppressive windowless wall of the Banco de la República building, began the Parque Santander. Later, remembering this moment, Mallarino would wonder if that was when he thought of the day Ricardo Rendón died. It's possible, he'd tell himself later, that he hadn't been conscious of it at that moment, for his attention was on the agreeable pressure of Magdalena's arm on his arm, on the scent of her hair, on the voice able to say, with that unpredictable sweetness, those things that pierced him to the marrow: *I had hoped, my dear, that it wouldn't occur to you,* for example, or also this other one: *We don't have time for this anymore.* But it had to be then, he would think, because it was just after pronouncing those words, there where you can see the sunshades of the shoe-shine stands, that he stopped in the middle of the sidewalk and, without marveling at the miracle, remembered once more those events he knew by heart although he'd never witnessed them.

He remembered the Chaplin film that Rendón went to see the night before, and also the profound but discreet depression overwhelming him during those days, and also the conversation with the managing editor of *El Tiempo*

and the suggestion to go and rest in a clinic. Mallarino remembered all that, and also the blue pencil drawings that
Rendón left at the newspaper office, beside the two recently published volumes of his caricatures, and in his
memory Rendón left the office after ten in the evening and
went into La Gran Vía, where he listened to music, drank
aguardiente, and joked with the bartender, then arrived at
his house on Eighteenth Street before midnight, sad but
not drunk, yet certainly tired. Mallarino remembered him
planning, sleeplessly, his caricature for the next day; also
him waking up and talking to his mother about what he
had planned. Rendón went out, dressed as usual in full
mourning, and Mallarino remembered him standing for a
short time at the corner of Seventh Avenue and then going
into La Gran Vía. In his memory, Rendón orders a Ger-
mania beer; he receives it on a tray; he lights a cigarette. He
thinks of Clarisa, the young girl he'd fallen in love with in
Medellín, so many years ago, and relives the displeasure
and the girl's parents' protest; he thinks of Clarisa and her
heroic stubbornness, her pregnancy, her forced confine-
ment, her illness and death. He finishes his beer, takes out
his pencil and draws one last picture (a diagram of straight
lines calculating the path of a bullet penetrating the skull),
writes those seven words that Mallarino remembers so
well, *I beg not to be taken home*, and then points the barrel
of his Colt .25 at his temple. Mallarino remembers him

doing what nobody ever saw: shooting himself. He remembers the head falling heavily to the table and the tray bouncing with a metallic jangling, the lips split by the blow and a broken tooth, the blood that begins to spill out (the blood that looks black running over the old wooden surface), and then he remembers him arriving at Doctor Manuel Vicente Peña's clinic, and remembers the doctor writing his report, choosing those words that Mallarino saw as if in black-and-white: *stertorous breathing, subcutaneous hematoma, hemorrhage in mouth, right parietal lobe.* The doctors perform a trephination of the cranium to alleviate the pressure of the blood and a strong viscous spurt lands on the white floor. Mallarino remembers it, and remembers the exact time of death, six-twenty in the evening. He remembered all that and heard Magdalena say: "We don't have time for this anymore."

Mallarino understood that it would be futile to insist, and that the suggestion had been a mistake. He understood other things as well, but these things were beyond immediate words, were on a terrain of intuition similar to that of faith. He felt tired, a sudden and treacherous tiredness like a child leaping onto his shoulders without warning. Then a movement distracted them: it was a man approaching with slow steps, his body leaning forward as though looking for a coin, and Mallarino remembered his features—the nose, the ears, the moustache white and gray like pigeon shit—before he spoke to them. The man stretched out a hand and Mallarino saw the stains of shoe polish and the dry skin, and his hand closed around the man's hand. The man's handshake was strong and solid. Mallarino also clasped firmly.

"Your Honor is the caricaturist," said the man. "I shined your shoes the other day and didn't even recognize you, how very sorry I am."

Mallarino stretched out his left arm and his watch appeared under the sleeve of his jacket. (He had thin wrists—Magdalena had always said he had womanly wrists—and when it was cold his watch strap loosened, sometimes swung all the way around, all to the immense amusement of Magdalena, who said that was exactly how women used to wear watches in the old days.) The dial moved slightly and rested against the prominence at the end of the ulna, the half sphere of bone that some people touch when they're worried. Mallarino took the face of his watch between thumb and forefinger. He thought he had time.

"Are you free?" he asked the bootblack.

"Of course, sir, by all means," said the man. "I'm so sorry not to have recognized you the other day. Imagine, sir: a personage like yourself."

Just after three, after saying good-bye to Magdalena on the university esplanade with a kiss on the lips and thinking that it might be the last one, after collecting his four-by-four from the parking lot on Twenty-fifth Street and driving north and then down the narrow road that ran through the Parque Nacional—a short but deceptive and sinuous road where one wouldn't want to be caught at night—after leaving the car in the sort of half-moon that constituted the very center of the park, Mallarino walked to the stone pool of the monument to Uribe Uribe, and from the edge he tried to pick out the travel agency on the other side of the street. According to the address, the place must be very close: it should be visible for anyone looking for it from there. Mallarino's eyes stung, as they always did when he came into town from his mountain refuge; now, even though he'd left the city center, the pollution was still in his tear ducts, and his eyes were still stinging. The afternoon was cloudy but it wouldn't rain now; there were no shadows on the sidewalks, but the open air of the park was warm and soft. The inhabitants of the park were feeling it too, the kite vendors, the children guarding parked cars or running around the pool, the young couples sitting on the grass. Mallarino felt they were looking at him as he looked across to the other side of the wide avenue, looking for

Cuéllar's widow's travel agency. He found the large white sign made of hard plastic, the word *Travels* in small italics, the word UNICORN in imposing capitals; he imagined the sign lit up when night had fallen, casting its light across the whole sidewalk. Beneath the right-hand edge, in front of the window but far from the entrance, was Samanta Leal.

She was waiting for him. Her posture had the studied inattention of waiting bodies: everyone who waits knows or thinks they might be seen at any moment, seen by the person they're waiting to meet, and their gestures, their mannerisms, the position of their legs and straightness of their back is never the same as it would be were they not waiting. Mallarino recognized the line of her shoulders and her hair, cut straight across her back like a sheet of copper, and he recognized the handbag, which was the same one out of which she'd pulled, the previous day, the tiny voice recorder—the dishonest recorder—the notebook, and the pen. She had, indeed, changed her clothes: this morning's white blouse was now a turquoise sweater that looked thin from a distance, and the skirt and tights were now replaced by trousers that gave her hips an established look, the air of a mature woman. Mallarino walked to the lights and waited for the traffic to stop. The cars and buses and trucks traveled in both directions, faces that passed in front of Mallarino's like projections on a screen, faces that existed in his life for a fleeting second and then sank back into nonexistence. Some faces looked at him with blank expressions before passing to the next face, that of some other pedestrian stopped on the busy sidewalk, another blank face to look at with the same blankness; others didn't even register his presence but looked farther away or closer, at the mountains, at the buildings, at an uninhabited portion of the visible world. Sometimes people want a rest from people. There was a time when he liked to be surrounded by people. Not anymore: he'd lost that. It was one of the many things this life of his had swallowed up. If only we knew ten percent, one percent, of the stories that go on in Bogotá! If only Mallarino could close his eyes and hear what those who surrounded him at that moment were thinking! But it wasn't possible; and we all go on like this, walking the sidewalks, stopping at the traffic lights, surrounded by people but always deaf.

There, stuck in the little crowd that was going to cross the street, he thought about what was about to happen. Maybe Rodrigo Valencia was right and all this was a mistake, a regrettable mistake. Maybe his prediction was correct: if he carried on with his intentions, if he went inside the travel agency with Samanta and talked to Cuéllar's widow or listened to Samanta, he would find a transformed world when he left: a world (and in the world, a country, and in the country, a city, and in the city, a newspaper) in which Mallarino would no longer be who he was now. After this conversation, no matter what it might contain, whatever might be said, the army of his enemies would come down on him without pity. Jackals, they were all jackals who had spent their lives waiting for such a declaration of vulnerability. Because they would find out, of course they would find out: whatever the conversation might contain and whatever might be said. It didn't matter what revelations came out in Cuéllar's widow's office, and it didn't even matter if there were any revelations at all, if the woman sent them away amid shouts and slaps without telling them anything new, or if she refused to speak, if she wielded the terrible revenge of silence: the silence that hurt Samanta so much, that for her would be the worst affront, the most distressing humiliation. All this was, in some measure, a humiliation for Samanta; but going through anxiety and daring and the affronting memory only to run up against silence would be the worst humiliation of all.

And even if it turned out that way, the jackals would find out and launch their attack. The important thing for them, thought Mallarino, would not be what had happened in the past but the caricaturist's current uncertainty and what that uncertainty revealed. They would also humiliate him, and that was all they'd need to humiliate him: the question would be enough, the simple question that was perhaps already forming on Samanta's tongue, that perhaps Samanta had been practicing all day, choosing the

JUAN GABRIEL VÁSQUEZ

words and the intonation to pronounce it, choosing even
the expression on her face to not look more defenseless
than necessary. Choosing her clothes, thought Mallarino,
yes, Samanta had surely selected her outfit thinking of the
question she was going to ask the widow of a dead congressman. For her there could be a variety of results, one
possibility among many or at least between two; not so for
him, for, no matter what happened at Unicorn Travels, on
his way out Mallarino would encounter his enemies of
forty years pointing at him, egging on a crazed mob ready
to judge him summarily and burn him at the stake, the
stake of capricious, changeable public opinion. Mallarino
the slanderer or simply the irresponsible, Mallarino the de-
stroyer of a man's life or simply the unpunished abuser of
the power of the media. Now he better understood what
had happened twenty-eight years ago, when he'd given
himself the pleasure of humiliating Congressman Adolfo
Cuéllar; he understood the fervor with which the public
had received the humiliation, that fervor disguised as indignation or condemnation. He had simply set the mechanism in motion, yes, had lit the fire and then warmed his
hands at the flames. . . . Now it was his turn. It didn't matter who had right on his or her side. Justice and injustice
didn't matter. There was only one thing the public liked
more than humiliation, and that was the humiliation of a
humiliator. That afternoon Mallarino was arriving to give

them that pleasure. What the dead man's wife said would make no difference whatsoever: if he decided to go inside Unicorn Travels, Mallarino would no longer have the moral authority he had at that moment but would become a cheap rumormonger, a sniper of other people's reputations. Someone like that cannot be out on the loose. Someone like that is dangerous.

And now the light turned red and the traffic stopped and Mallarino could cross the street, cut through that heavy heat that forms like a cloud in front of a line of cars at a Bogotá traffic light. "Samanta!" he shouted from the corner, like an impatient child. But he was fifty steps from her, fifty steps from Unicorn Travels and the door that would change his life, and he could not be expected to be patient, could not be expected to wait until he'd covered that distance before declaring his presence to Samanta Leal. "Samanta!" he shouted. She raised her head and turned in the direction of the shout and saw him; she lifted a timid but contented hand, waved it in the air, slowly at first and then enthusiastically, and something lit up in her face, and Mallarino thought that not even two days ago— the night of the ceremony, at the bar of the Teatro Colón, with a piece of plastic stuck on her little girl's tongue— had he seen her look so lovely. And if he could go back to the night of the ceremony, the glory of the speeches and the medals and the pats on the back? If he could, would he? No, he wouldn't, thought Mallarino, and he was surprised to find himself thinking that. Again Rodrigo Valencia's words appeared in his head, those impertinent words: *What good is it going to do?* What good is ruining a man's life, even if the man deserves ruin? What good is this power if nothing changed except the ruin of that man? Forty years: everyone had been congratulating him lately, and only now had Mallarino realized that his longevity was not a virtue but an insult; forty years, and nothing around him had changed. *I beg not to be taken home:* Mallarino peered at the phrase as one peers at a puddle of dark water, and he thought he saw something glistening at the bottom. Again he thought of the homage; he thought of the stamp, of his own face looking out of the frame with the ferocious serrated edges at him. All that was far behind him now, very far: here, on this sidewalk on Seventh Avenue at this hour of the Bogotá afternoon, all that began to form part of his memory, and could be forgotten. Would Mallarino manage to? The memory has a marvelous capacity to remember the forgotten, its existence and its stalking, and thus allow us to stay alert when we don't want to forget and to forget when we choose to. Freedom, freedom from the past: that's what Mallarino desired above all now.

There was no longer anything tying him to the past. The present was a weight and a nuisance, like an addiction

to a drug. The future, however, belonged to him. It was all
a question of seeing the future, of knowing how to see it
clearly, to divest ourselves for an instant of our propensity
for deceit—the deceit of others and of ourselves—and of
the thousand lies we tell ourselves about what might happen to us. It is necessary to lie to ourselves, of course, because no one can stand too much clairvoyance: How many
would want to know the date of their own death, for example, or foresee illness or misfortune? But now, arriving
to meet Samanta, seeing her so lovely in her turquoise
sweater, so solid against the blurry background of shop
windows and their reflections, her mouth half open, as if
singing a secret song, Mallarino suddenly understood that
he could do it: he understood that, even if he had no control over the moving, volatile past, he could remember
with total clarity his own future. Is that not what he did
each time he drew a caricature? He imagined a scene,
imagined a character, assigned him features, and wrote in
his head the epigram that would be like a stinger dipped
in honey, and after doing this he had to remember it to be
able to draw it: none of that had existed when he sat down
at his drafting table, and nevertheless Mallarino was able
to remember it, had to remember it to put it down on
paper. Yes, thought Mallarino, the White Queen was right:
it's a poor sort of memory that only works backwards.

And then, in a lightning flash of lucidity, he remembered himself returning that very evening to his house in the mountains, climbing the stairs to his studio, and sitting down in his chair, and he remembered exactly what he will do. He will glance over the cuttings pinned up on his cork wall: the Colombian president, the Latin American liberator, the German pope. He will turn on the lamp, take a sheet of letterhead notepaper out of the filing cabinet, pick up his fountain pen, and write today's date and, under the date, the name Rodrigo Valencia. *By means of this letter (that's how you say it, isn't it? so as to be formal and pretty; I like things to be well presented) I wish to notify you of my unconditional resignation (a little dramatic, I know, but that's how it is, what can we do) from the newspaper that you, with such good fortune, have published during recent years (fewer than the number of years I have spent drawing cartoons, it must be said). I take this decision after long and intense consultations with my pillow and other authorities, and hasten to emphasize that my decision, as well as being unconditional, is irrevocable, definitive, and all those long words. So don't bother wearing yourself out, brother, you'll get nothing by insisting.* He will go to the kitchen for a large plastic rubbish bag, black with an orange band, and begin chucking into it bottles of ink, blades, his pencil holder (the cut-off end of a rain stick) and with it charcoals, seven different kinds of leads, an unused spatula, and a collection of nibs and brushes, well combed like the members of a school choir, and all would end up at the bottom of the bag. One by one, Mallarino will take the drawers out of his filing cabinet and empty them into the bag, and he will enjoy the sound of paper falling in cascades to the bottom and the static produced by its friction with the bag. He will pull off the skinny liberator and the haggard pope, the recently elected president and recently killed guerrilla, and throw them in the bag. He will take two steps back, will look at the empty spaces appearing in the wake of his hand, clearings opening up in the middle of the dense jungle. He will take the slogan about the stinger and honey down off the wall and put it in the bag. He will take Daumier's caricature down and put it in the bag.

And then he'll do the same with all the rest.

AUTHOR'S NOTE

Reputations is a work of fiction; any resemblance to reality is purely coincidental. Having satisfied the convention of stating this disclaimer, which no reader should take completely seriously, I wish to thank those who gave me their time and offered me anecdotes from their lives or ideas about their trade, especially Vladimir Flórez ("Vladdo") and Andrés Rábago ("El Roto"). Other caricaturists lent me, unknowingly, more or less concrete information, and I'd also like to recognize my debt—more ambiguous and less direct –to Antonio Caballero, Héctor Osuna, and José María Pérez González ("Peridis"). In writing the lines about the death of Ricardo Rendón, I found the book *5 en humor*, by María Teresa Ronderos, very useful. I would also like to acknowledge my unpayable debt to Jorge Ruffi-nelli and Héctor Hoyos, both of Stanford University, for the invitation and hospitality that allowed me to finish this novel in an apartment on Oak Creek Drive in Palo Alto, California. Finally, I'd like once more to give myself the pleasure (and put on record the infinite good fortune) of finishing a book by writing the name Mariana.

A NOTE ON THE AUTHOR

JUAN GABRIEL VÁSQUEZ was born in Bogotá in 1973. He studied Latin American literature at the Sorbonne and has translated works by E. M. Forster and Victor Hugo, among others, into Spanish. His previous books have won the International IMPAC Dublin Literary Award, the Alfaguara Novel Prize, the Gregor von Rezzori Prize, and the Prix Roger Caillois; he has been shortlisted for the *Independent* Foreign Fiction Prize. *Reputations* received a Royal Spanish Academy prize in 2014. His books have been published in twenty-six languages and in forty countries. After sixteen years in France, Belgium, and Spain, he now lives in Bogotá.

A NOTE ON THE TRANSLATOR

ANNE McLEAN has translated works by many Spanish and Latin American authors, including Héctor Abad, Javier Cercas, Carmen Martín Gaite, Julio Cortázar, Ignacio Martínez de Pisón, Enrique Vila-Matas, and Tomás Eloy Martínez. Her previous translations have been awarded the *Independent* Foreign Fiction Prize, the Premio Valle Inclán, and the International IMPAC Dublin Literary Award. She lives in Toronto.